The All Hallows' Icon

A Harry Fox Origin Story

Andrew Clawson

Golden Idol Publishing

Contents

Chapter 1

Florence, Italy

A giant nearly crushed Harry Fox flat.

"Watch it!" Harry barked as he jumped back to avoid a muscle-bound arm and offered a few choice words. The man stopped. He turned to face Harry. Who began to regret his choice of words.

The big brute leaned toward Harry just as a long selfie stick pushed between them and a pair of Asian women chattering excitedly swept through without a glance at either man. Harry Fox knew the sound of opportunity knocking. He took his chance and darted behind a group of tourists gathered around a guide speaking French. Harry only turned once those dozen tourists stood between him and the big guy, looking back to find the man offering Harry one final glower before he went on his way.

"This piazza's huge and you manage to run into me," Harry muttered to himself. Softly, taking no chance the big guy might hear him. "Lucky I have business to handle."

Even Harry didn't believe his bluster. He headed across the *Piazza della Signora*, the open square fronting the fourteenth-century town hall of Florence. The scent of rich espresso ran across his nose while conversations in multiple languages could be heard around him. Harry narrowed his gaze on one statue ahead. A statue of a stark-naked man with a head of curly hair and a body known across the globe. It was a copy of the original sculpture nearby.

"Afternoon, David." Harry spoke to the statue as he approached. "You see my guy?"

The statue did not reply. Harry slowed as he approached the giant replica, looking at and then past every single person around David. Not at their faces. He looked at their heads. Or rather, what sat atop their heads. A flash of yellow caught his attention. "Found you."

Harry Fox had come to Florence to make a purchase. The seller had promised to wear a bright yellow hat so Harry wouldn't miss him in the crowd. A crowd Harry insisted on being in when this deal went down. Not because he didn't trust this seller. But because his dad always told him not to trust anyone.

A couple took pictures in front of the replica of David as Harry circled around to stand in front of the man in the yellow hat, now at David's rear. The tall pedestal holding the statue cast yellow hat in shadow. A metal case that could have held a guitar rested against the pedestal. Yellow hat kept two hands on the case. A case he had good reason to keep close, for what it contained would soon bring him a lot of money.

Harry looked to either side before posing a question. "Did you come alone?"

Oskar Bulka, he of the yellow hat, nodded. "I did."

Harry nodded to the case. "Open it," Harry said.

Oskar flicked several latches and then indicated for Harry to come closer. "I do not think you want all these people to see it too," Oskar said. "I wish we did not meet here."

What Oskar wanted was not Harry's concern. "Keep it out of sight," Harry said.

Oskar did as asked. Their bodies shielded the case from view as Harry opened it far enough that he could see inside. He drew in a breath, then let it out in a slow whistle. "It's gorgeous."

Three feet of steel gleamed. Nestled inside the velvet-lined case, the sword looked sharp enough to inflict serious damage. Not bad for a piece of metal crafted nearly two thousand years ago. Harry opened the lid further and angled his head to get a better look at the inscriptions on the blade's center. His lips moved silently as he translated the Latin. "Exactly as you described it," Harry said before he closed the case and reached into his coat pocket, coming out with a thick envelope. "Fifty thousand euros, as agreed."

Oskar put the envelope inside his jacket, furtively checking the stack of five-hundred-euro notes for several moments before tucking them away. Not that Harry watched him. He was too busy staring at the sword.

A Roman *spatha,* the straight sword favored by heavy infantry in the Roman Empire. This sword had clearly never seen combat. Harry could have picked up a similar sword for a fraction of the price without leaving Brooklyn, yet he'd traveled across an ocean to meet a Polish dealer while carrying a small fortune in cash to buy this specific sword. Why? Because this weapon had been a gift from an emperor. Constantine the Great, who reigned during the fourth century, had ordered this sword crafted as a gift to the pagan tribal leader of what would eventually become Great Britain, though at the time it was a wild and untamed land populated by various tribes who constantly warred with each other. Yes, Julius Caesar had invaded Britain some two hundred years before, and future Roman leaders continued the quest to subjugate the Britons with varying degrees of success, but when faced with Constantine's legions the native Britons had decided to give peace a try. They came to him seeking peace, offering gifts along with their promises, so Constantine had offered his own gift in return.

This *spatha*. Constantine told the pagan king that this gift, a sword unlike any other, was the Sword of Fionn mac Cumhaill. A clever move, naming the sword after a legendary myth in which Fionn slew a fire-breathing assailant one day each year—a day held dear by the Britons. The sword was decorated with symbols of the pagan holiday Samhain. Although this sword represented the promise of peace, history, however, would prove this promise false. This *spatha* marked the beginning of the end of the Britons' way of life. It was a deception they did not see coming.

Oskar's voice pulled Harry from his thoughts. "We have a deal?"

Harry closed the case. "We do." He stuck one hand out. "Pleasure doing—"

"Give me the case."

A shadow fell over Harry as a man stepped close to him. Harry looked up. All the way up until he found the face of a man he'd been hoping to never see again. The giant who'd nearly run him over. Fire burned in Harry's gut. "Piss off."

The man stood a foot taller than Harry. He did not piss off, but reached under his shirt and put one meaty hand on the grip of a very big pistol. "I said give me the case."

A small part of Harry's brain not shouting at him to run noted the man's Italian accent even as the guy spoke English. "You want it?" Harry asked. "Fine." He made a show of reaching slowly into the case. "You don't need the gun. I'm not getting shot over this thing."

The big man's hand came ever-so-slightly off the pistol. Harry glanced at Oskar. Every bit of color had drained from his face. *Oskar knows this guy.* Harry played a hunch. “You’re the guy I outbid.” He had no idea if there had been a bidding war.

“Wrong.” The big man shook his head. “He refused to sell.”

Oskar found a shadow of his voice. “I do not sell to fascists.” His eyes narrowed and he spat at the ground. “Werewolf scum.”

The big man growled but kept his eyes on Harry. “Hand it over.”

Fascists? Werewolf? Harry filed that away. That could matter if he survived this. “Easy,” Harry said, his hand now inside the case. “You can have it.” His fingers wrapped around the sword’s handle and he lifted it free. “Just don’t—”

He whipped the blade out and sliced at the big man’s hand. Steel flashed, the big man moved, and Harry’s arm shuddered as though he’d sliced into a brick wall. Too late he realized the flat of the blade, instead of a sharp edge, had smashed into the big man’s arm. Big man shouted, the gun went flying, and before Harry could react, the big guy’s other arm came out of nowhere. An open palm smashed into the side of Harry’s skull and sent him stumbling toward Oskar. Harry slammed into the Polish seller as a grisly noise sounded.

The sword was buried halfway into Oskar’s stomach. Osker’s eyes bulged and his mouth hung open as he slumped, lifeless, against the pedestal. Movement in the corner of Harry’s eye made him duck. The big man’s fist whizzed through the air above his head as Harry pulled the sword free from Oskar’s corpse. He turned to find not a single person even looking at the unfolding disaster, so he ran.

Directly into a group of tourists not ten feet away. German curses filled the air as people flew in all directions. Harry rolled as he hit the ground, popped up to his feet and kept moving. A glance back found the big man rumbling through, hot on Harry’s tail.

Thick white columns flashed by on one side as he raced through a narrow street. Metal scaffolding groaned on the other side. Harry sprinted past clusters of pedestrians as the sound of his footsteps echoed off the tall buildings to either side; the big man kept close. A woman pointed at Harry, her mouth open. *The sword.* His hand still clasped the bloodied weapon for anyone to see. He jammed it inside his jacket without breaking stride. Hand-drawn caricatures propped on easels nearly went flying as he veered around yet another barricade cordoning off a construction zone. Beeping sounded as Harry looked back. Beeping he ignored.

Until he ran headfirst into the side of a reversing van. The impact tossed him backwards, his world spinning as the ground raced up and crashed into his backside. He bounced up as pain coursed through his entire body, everything aching as he regained his feet, ignored the now honking horn and bolted around the front of the van toward an archway beyond. Two security guards stood at the head of a queue of people lined up behind the columns. They never even looked over at the pursuit.

Harry glanced at the line again. *The Uffizi.* People were waiting to enter Florence's world-renowned gallery, where the real David could be seen. Harry raced beneath an archway. The Arno River blocked his path ahead. He hung a hard right, his boots skidding on the stone street as he took the turn without slowing. Loud cursing and shouting followed moments later when the big man ignored the laws of physics and tried to make the same turn without success.

An elderly couple eating gelato stared wide-eyed as Harry raced past. A colorful graffiti tag on a rolling metal door flashed by on one side, the river sparkling ahead as the sun came out on the other. Harry swerved around a slow-moving cyclist and saw what waited. Closed-in shops running across a bridge known across the globe. The Ponte Vecchio.

The only Florentine bridge not destroyed in World War II, it had jewelers, art dealers and souvenir sellers running its length on either side. What caught Harry's eye as he turned onto the bridge was a way to save his neck.

A metal fire escape affixed to a shop on one end led to a window on the top floor. Harry leapt up and grabbed the lowest rung, which was retracted well above ground level. The big guy shouldn't be able to jump that high. Get to the top, lose the brute and be—*bang.*

The bottom part of the metal ladder slid down to ground level. Harry scrambled up to the first landing and turned to pull the ladder up after him, out of reach.

Too late. The big man had hold of one of the lower rungs and was on his way up.

Harry pounded up to the second landing, his legs shouting in protest as the metal rattled and the big guy kept pace. Harry made it to the next section of the ladder, which led to the top landing. A closed window waited there. Harry's gaze went to the gutter above him. It looked sturdy. *This better work.*

Harry jumped, grabbed hold of the gutter and pulled. The gutter held. He pulled himself up, swinging his torso over the edge and kicking to get one leg on the roof. One leg made it. The other did not.

"Got you!"

The big guy grabbed hold of Harry's dangling leg. Harry kicked; the man held on, then pulled. Harry's muscles burned as he fought to keep hold of the terra cotta roof tiles. *Forget this.* His jaw went tight as he let his other leg dangle back over the roof edge, pulled his foot up, and smashed it down about where the big man's head should be. Nothing but air. He slid a bit lower, pulled his leg back and gave it a second go. Direct hit. The big guy howled as he let go of Harry's leg, and Harry whipped himself up onto the rooftop.

A view of Florence stretched out around him. The Arno's waters dazzled in the sunlight; he could see a single boat puttering down the river and pedestrians on the sidewalk. Harry turned and ran.

And immediately slipped. A roof tile shot out from under his foot and he crashed down, getting up a beat later and trying to run again. He made it one step before the big man grabbed hold of his collar. Harry reached into his jacket, grabbed the sword and spun, using the flat side of the blade like a club.

The *thud* of metal hitting bone reached Harry's ears a moment before the big man fell sideways over the roof edge. Harry leapt as the sword clattered across the tiles and followed the big man over the edge.

"No!" Harry cried out as the sword slipped from his grasp and chased the falling man into the river, slicing through the water to vanish from sight.

The closest group of pedestrians began to shout, pointing at the man splashing around in the water. Harry kept low as he spun around and crawled toward the bridge side of the roof to where a drainpipe waited. He flipped over the gutter edge, grabbed hold of the drainpipe and descended hand-over-hand until he could drop onto the Ponte Vecchio bridge.

He landed directly beside a woman wearing enough diamonds to ransom a duke. Harry dipped his chin. "Afternoon."

The woman gaped as Harry turned and calmly walked into the crowd. First, he needed to get away from here. Next, he had to do what he really didn't want to do: Call his dad. Harry shook his head as he moved. *Dad's not going to like this.*

Chapter 2

Florence, Italy

Nobody paid attention to the bedraggled man sitting on a stone bench by the Leonardo da Vinci Museum on a narrow street in Florence. The man leaned back against the museum wall, eyes closed, a phone pressed to his ear. Only when a passing woman walked too close and bumped against his leg did he open his eyes, shooting to his feet with a crazed look. The woman backed hastily away. The man looked dangerous. The sort of man anyone with good sense left alone.

"Sorry," Harry said into the phone, resuming his seat. "What were you saying?"

"Are you safe?"

"I'm fine, Dad." Harry rubbed his forehead. "Just a little jumpy."

Fred Fox was Harry's father and knew a thing or two about how relic deals could go wrong. "Perhaps you should get out of Florence," Fred said. "You have no idea who that man was."

"He only wanted the sword," Harry said.

"Maybe," Fred said patiently. "But I suspect that's not all."

"Why?" Silence greeted his question. A silence Harry understood. "What aren't you telling me?"

Harry and Fred had run through this deal together before he ever left Brooklyn. They had covered the sword's history, made contingency plans, all of it. The sort of background and planning a professional relic hunter would work through with certainty.

"One moment." The line seemed to go dead in Harry's ear. His dad had muted the phone. Harry waited.

"Hello, Harry."

A new, familiar voice filled Harry's ear. He involuntarily sat up straighter. "Mr. Morello."

"It's Vincent, please." Soft tones from a man who was anything but. "I understand you had a complication."

Pretty forgiving, considering Harry had just lost over fifty thousand dollars of Vincent's money. "I promise I'll find out who he was." A lame response and he knew it.

"There is no need," Vincent said. "I know who he was. And I know why he came."

Harry knew to keep quiet.

Vincent's next words caught him off guard. "Describe the man."

Harry frowned, pulling up the big man in his mind's eye. "Big guy. Really big. Spoke English with an Italian accent."

"Did he hear you speak English before he spoke?"

Vincent Morello had become the crime boss of New York by noticing the little things. "I don't believe so," Harry said. "That bothered me."

"It should. Go on."

"He had a gun," Harry said. "Which suggests he has connections. Handguns aren't easy to get in Italy."

"He has resources," Vincent said. "The man is part of a terrible organization."

Harry did not point out that the same could be said about the Morello family.

"He and his godless associates have one aim," Vincent continued. "To destroy that which is most dear. Our faith."

Family and faith stood at the center of Vincent Morello's life. Except when profits were involved. Then faith took a distant third. Harry would keep that thought to himself.

"They're trying to destroy the Catholic Church," Harry said aloud.

"May they never succeed," Vincent said. Harry could picture the old man crossing himself as he spoke. "I only learned of their possible involvement today, after you left for the sale in Florence."

A memory flashed to life. "The seller said something to this guy before," Harry hesitated. "Before he died. First, he called the big guy a fascist. Then it sounded like he called him *werewolf scum.* Which can't be right."

A sigh. "It is correct."

"Why call the guy a werewolf?" Harry asked. "He was big enough to be a monster, but a werewolf? That makes no sense."

"Oskar spoke of real monsters," Vincent said.

What? "Is werewolf the name of this organization?" Harry guessed.

"I always knew you were an intelligent young man. That is correct," Vincent said. "The man is part of a terrorist organization that calls itself *Werewulfs*." He spelled it out for Harry. "Their roots are deep and dark."

Fred Fox spoke up. "Werewulf, however you spell it, is a name used by various fascist groups across Europe. The term comes from a Nazi plan developed near the end of World War Two aimed at creating resistance forces to hinder Allied efforts as they advanced into Germany.

Nazis took the name from an old German novel about peasants who stood up to marauding invaders."

"Not the werewolf I pictured."

"The main character was named Wulf, and the association with terrifying mythical creatures served a purpose. It inspired fear. The same purpose these terrorists have today."

"And this modern group wants to take down the Catholic Church," Harry said. "What does this have to do with Constantine's sword?"

Vincent responded. "You will learn more in your meeting."

Harry shot up from the bench. "What meeting?"

"A car is waiting for you beside the Leonardo da Vinci Museum entrance," Vincent said. "A black sedan. The man inside wishes to speak with you."

"Who is he?"

"A friend," Vincent said. "You would do me a favor by listening to him."

"Of course." One didn't turn down a request for a favor from Vincent Morello. "What do I need to know?"

"He will tell you everything," Vincent said. "You can trust this man."

"Understood." Harry looked past the trickle of people moving into and out of the museum entrance. A black sedan idled at the curb not fifty feet away. "I'll be in touch." He clicked off, stood and walked to the vehicle. The driver's door opened as Harry approached and a man stepped out. Harry hesitated when he spotted the simple white collar. *That's an expensive ride for a priest.*

The priest opened the rear door and motioned for Harry to enter. Harry ducked his head down, narrowing his gaze into the rear seat where the rapidly fading fall sunlight did not reach. A man sat in the shadows. The radio played a talk show softly in the background.

"Hello, Mr. Fox. Please join me."

Harry blinked as his vision adjusted. The idea of a priest being driven around in a flashy Mercedes sedan had surprised him. Now, he knew why. Another man sat in the back seat, this one a Cardinal of the Church. "Good afternoon, Your Eminence."

"Please excuse my formal attire," the man said as Harry sat down and the door closed behind him. "I did not have time to change."

The short man beside Harry wore a robe of brilliant red. His skin had the tone of a man who had been born in the Italian countryside and spent many hours in the sun. The hand he offered Harry told another story—that of a man who now spent his days at a desk. The smooth skin of a man who exerted influence through a pen, not a sword.

Harry shook the man's hand. "Call me Harry."

"Harry." The man offered a genuine smile. "My name is Roberto Maldini."

"Nice to meet you, Cardinal Maldini."

"Roberto will suffice," he said. "Thank you for agreeing to meet with me."

As if he had a choice. "What's going on?" Harry asked. "Today's been tough and I have no idea why."

Roberto spoke in rapid Italian to the driver, who pulled the car into racing traffic with practiced ease. "First, tell me about the incident that occurred near the Palazzo Vecchio. And continued onto the Ponte Vecchio, I believe."

"Correct on both counts," Harry said. "It started when I tried to buy a relic—a sword."

Cardinal Maldini listened as Harry recounted the sale, the interruption, the attack and the subsequent chase. The car radio stayed at a low volume the entire time, playing what sounded to Harry like a podcast. The Cardinal didn't react when Harry related the fight atop a bridge, nor when he told how the Arno River had claimed Constantine's sword. "I lost the sword," Harry finished. "I didn't want to hang around for the police or more trouble."

Roberto's fingers drummed on the leather seat between them. "His name is Demetrio."

"The man who attacked me?"

"Yes. Demetrio Costa. He goes by Demeter. He is well known to the *carabinieri.*"

Made sense the Italian police force knew of the guy. "Demeter is the guy I outbid to buy the sword. He somehow knew where Oskar and I set the exchange and he decided to take the sword.

"It's an historic piece, sure. But worth killing over? He seemed almost anxious to use that gun even before I pulled out the sword."

"A sword against a gun?" Roberto lifted an eyebrow. "I am not certain I would have the courage."

Harry's jaw tightened. "It wasn't his sword."

"Admirable." More drumming while Harry digested that backhanded compliment. "Demeter would have killed ten men to get that sword. Do you recall the inscription?"

Harry's heart rate picked up. "Oskar sent me pictures of the sword during our negotiation, but none of them gave a clear image of the inscription. I guess he intentionally blurred it out."

"And you were not as interested in the writing as in the sword itself."

"Constantine's sword is valuable no matter what's written on it," Harry said. He did not admit he should have demanded clear images.

Rookie mistake. "I only saw it for a few seconds," Harry said. "I do know it had a name."

"The Sword of Fionn mac Cumhaill." Roberto turned to face Harry. "You know the legend?"

"Fionn was a man in Irish mythology who slew a fire-breathing man named Aillen. He killed Aillen because he burned the Irish capital of Tara every year on Samhain."

"Tara is now a hill in Ireland."

Harry smirked. "So I've heard."

"Constantine crafted the sword as a gift of peace," Roberto said.

"I'm guessing this story doesn't have a happy ending. Who received the gift?"

"An Irish pagan leader who had given Constantine a gift first. Also intended as a gift of peace."

"How'd that work out for the pagans?"

Roberto didn't take the bait. "The Irish pagans gave Constantine a symbol of their faith. A statue." Roberto looked toward the windshield ahead as they slowed for an intersection. "A statue of a creature you know."

Harry knew the sword had been a gift and it had ties to Irish mythology. He didn't know it had been part of a gift exchange. "I've read Irish mythology. They have any number of creatures."

"None of which is the one I mean. This statue depicted a creature from Greek myth, not Irish."

Greek myth? "The Irish pagans had heard Greek stories and adopted them."

Roberto nodded his agreement. "The statue depicted Medusa."

One of three Gorgon sisters, Medusa possessed a stony stare and head of writhing snakes that had struck fear in humankind for ages. That she would represent a pagan deity beyond Greece did not surprise Harry. That she came as a symbol of peace baffled him. "I bet it got Constantine's attention."

"The pagan Irish had Rome's attention long before Constantine. The word of our Lord had not spread to the Irish lands, and Constantine wished to save their immortal souls."

"Did the Irish want to be saved?"

Roberto's lips tightened, only for an instant. "No man is infallible. We all make mistakes." Roberto inclined his head toward a speaker embedded in the door. "The listeners of this program, for example."

The man whose voice Harry had heard when he first sat in the car was still talking. "Who is this guy?" Harry asked. Only now did he pay attention to what the man said. "He's talking about some kind of disease."

"The disease of which he speaks is the Church. This man is a fervent nationalist and he despises anyone who does not look or think like him."

"Doesn't sound like the sort of program you'd listen to."

Roberto lifted a finger in response. "Listen."

Harry leaned closer and caught a few sentences. "Something about snakes and a sign from the true gods," Harry said. "What's he talking about?"

"Time will tell. Soon, I am afraid."

Roberto's face told Harry the bigot on the radio worried him. Harry shook his head and went back to the reason he sat here. "I came here to get a sword, and you're telling me the Church made a mistake. I don't see how that connects to the sword," Harry said. "A sword that's at the bottom of a river. You planning to dredge it? If so, that sword is more valuable than I realized."

"It *is* more valuable than you know, and we have no intention of dredging the river." Roberto spoke toward their driver. "The case, please." The priest in the front seat picked up a case that was sitting beside him and handed it back to them. "Take it," Roberto said. "What is inside will answer some of your questions."

Harry noted how much this new case resembled the one Oskar had carried. He set it on his lap and opened the clasps. "Holy sh—smokes." The half-offered curse hung in the air as Harry stared at an impossibility. "It's the same sword," Harry said. "There are two of them?"

"Constantine presented one to the Irish pagans," Roberto said. "He kept one for himself. Why? The sword is more than a symbol. It is a message. A message too valuable to lose."

"The message I read talked about paths and"—he struggled to recall—"bonfires. I only saw a piece of it, and it made no sense." Harry crossed his arms. "Sounds like you know more."

Roberto gestured to the sword Harry held. "This is identical to the one you wielded earlier today. Read it."

Harry looked down, and for the second time today, beheld a message crafted two thousand years earlier. He read the Latin script, then translated to English aloud. "*The true bonds holding all together begin at the fire of Samhain.*"

Harry flipped the sword over. "Same message on both sides of the blade." He took a breath, then closed his eyes, opened them, and really *looked* at the sword. "Tell me if I'm way off base." Roberto didn't respond. "The fact you're telling me to read this means it's more than I suspect. Constantine had an ulterior motive. Which is probably the least surprising thing I'll hear all day."

Roberto had the decency to nod. "Go on."

"The Catholic Church isn't known for peace. It's known for conquest." Again, Roberto didn't argue. "There's a message behind the message." Harry frowned. "And that message can be found at the fire of Samhain."

Harry looked up. Roberto motioned for him to continue. "In Irish mythology, Samhain is the day when passages or doorways to the afterlife open and spirits can return to the world of the living. Many versions of this idea occur across history in every civilization." Harry's voice quickened as his thoughts came into focus. Once more, he felt the thrill of discovery he'd experienced for the first time earlier this year on his first solo relic hunt. "Samhain occurred at the end of October when temperatures dropped and the nights grew long. Irish pagans lit bonfires for both practical and symbolic reasons. Practically speaking, fire pushed back the dark and kept the people warm. Symbolically, it warded off malevolent spirits that emerged from the world of the dead."

Harry turned the sword over in his hands. "This message talks about fire. Not just any fire. *The* fire."

The sword gleamed as he studied it. *The fire.* One fire that stood above all others. Harry's head snapped up. "Where was the biggest Samhain celebration in Ireland during Constantine's reign? That's what I need to know." Harry tapped the sword's message. "My gut says we need to look there."

Roberto hardly moved. "You seem certain. The largest Samhain ceremonies at the time took place near cairns."

"Tombs." Harry snapped his fingers. "The dead would return to the living world from the place they'd departed it." Harry frowned. "Any idea how many cairns exist in Ireland?"

"Thousands have been discovered."

Harry slumped back into his seat. "There's a real chance whatever cairn this sword references has never been found. If I'm even on the right track."

The sword twisted in his hands. Harry's gaze narrowed. He sat back up. "The engraving on the pommel is a Latin word." He managed to angle the weapon without stabbing himself. A decorative engraving ran across the bottom of the pommel. An engraving he couldn't help but notice resembled a Latin word. "It's the word *Calvaria*," Harry said. "Latin for skull. Written in a very elegant script." He frowned. "The C doesn't align with the rest of the word." Sloppy craftsmanship on a beautiful sword made no sense. Harry ran his thumb over the misaligned letter and inspiration struck. "Unless that's the point."

The etched letters weren't embedded in the pommel. They rose from it, slightly above the surface, tickling the rough skin on his thumb as he rubbed it. He pressed hard on the *C*, as though he were trying to push it up to align with the rest of the letters.

He nearly dropped the sword when the letter moved, sliding into place with a *click*. "It moves."

"I know."

Harry looked up from the pommel. "You *knew* it moved?"

"Vincent was correct about you," Roberto said. "You are quite good at uncovering the past. The Church has known the secret of Constantine's sword since the turn of the first millennium. It took seven hundred years to discover the hidden mechanism. You found it in seven minutes."

"Why didn't you tell me?"

Roberto lifted a hand. "Curiosity." Harry didn't respond as Roberto pointed to the sword. "Look closely at the crosspiece. You will find it has changed."

A metal guard perpendicular to the blade protected the hand during combat. Harry turned the sword around to discover a small section of the cross guard had come loose. "It's a compartment," Harry said. He drew in a sharp breath. "There's a rolled piece of paper inside."

Chapter 3

Harry removed a rolled piece of what turned out to be leather. "There's writing on it," he said as he unrolled it. "No, it's a drawing." He glanced up at Roberto. "Which you already know. It's a drawing of a skull."

He held the image up for Roberto to see. An outline of a skull had been sketched on the leather, its rounded eye sockets and the empty spot for a nose unmistakable. "The jaw isn't connected," Harry said. "And it looks too narrow for the head."

The area where the jaw should have been connected below the ears had been left blank, leaving the upper portion of the skull disconnected from the lower. "That's odd," Harry said. "I bet you know why."

"No. I am afraid the mystery of this skull eludes me."

"Then I bet you know more than you're telling me."

"Some information is better left in the dark."

What was this guy's deal? "Maybe you don't know about this skull drawing, but you know more about the situation, the hidden compartment. All of it. Tell me."

"I will share what I know."

"Demeter and the werewolf organization," Harry said. "Start with that."

"Demeter is part of a fascist group intent on destroying the Catholic Church. The group's name ties to National Socialism, not to mythical creatures."

"Where are they based?"

"Italy. There may be smaller groups in other countries, but the main group, and the men who most concern us, are in and around Rome."

"How did Demeter find me in Florence?"

"I do not know."

"How did you know to find me here?"

"Through my relationship with Vincent Morello."

Fine. "What about the Medusa statue and the sword? Seems like they're tied together."

"I do not have the entire story."

"What *do* you know?"

"Emperor Constantine was the first Christian Roman emperor," Roberto began. "Sylvester the First was the Holy Father at the time, and Constantine had a steadfast resolve to help others see the light."

"You mean to convert them."

"Yes. Pagan beliefs persisted across Europe, resulting in violent clashes between the faiths. Constantine wished to end the conflict."

"He wanted to win the holy war."

"A war that continues to this day," Roberto said. "Constantine wished to avoid unnecessary violence in this pursuit, so he contacted Pope Sylvester."

"You sure about that?" Harry asked. Roberto's silence made it clear he wasn't. "Fine." Harry waved a hand. "Constantine contacted Sylvester to discuss battle plans, so to speak." Harry wasn't sold yet, but he went with it. "To plan for the peaceful conversion of the pagans."

Harry watched as they passed by where he'd been picked up a short while ago. It seemed they were going in circles. "What was their plan?"

"The Irish pagan leaders understood that to fight against the Romans was a losing proposition. They came to Rome to present Constantine with a peace offering."

"The Medusa statue."

"Correct. In return, Constantine crafted this sword and presented it to the Irish pagans as a symbol of peace." Here Roberto turned away. "The sword is a window showing the future."

Harry connected dots he hadn't seen. "You mean the skull somehow foretold the future?"

"I believe it did, and still does."

"But you're not certain."

"I am not. The truth behind this sword and what it represents has been lost over time."

"You think it was more than a message of peace?"

"That is where my knowledge ends." Roberto said something softly in Italian that Harry didn't catch, and their vehicle made a turn. "The Werewolves have secretly declared war on the Church and escalated anti-Church activity."

"Are they only making trouble for Catholics, or for all religions?"

"As of now their focus is on Catholicism. If they succeed, their focus will surely expand against other faiths."

Nothing good would come of that. Harry hefted the sword as realization dawned. "Demeter didn't want this so he could show it off. He wanted this so he could *find the message inside.*"

"My thoughts exactly," Roberto said. "That is also the conclusion of Church intelligence services. The Werewolf Group wishes to use that sword to uncover the truth."

"The truth about what?"

Roberto twisted a golden ring on one finger. "What I am about to share with you is in the strictest confidence."

"Who would believe me even if I told them?"

More ring twisting. "I have your word?"

Harry didn't even try to convince himself this was a bad idea. "I promise."

One final twist before Roberto looked up. "Constantine and Sylvester the First struck an agreement: to accelerate the pagan adoption of Christianity."

"Did the Irish get a say in this agreement?"

"Details are scarce." Roberto lifted a hand to beg patience. "It is my understanding that, by design, no written records were made of the arrangements."

A fair point. If you're up to no good, why create evidence? "What else do you know?" Harry asked. "Why tell me about all of this?" Roberto's contact with him was rooted in a connection to Vincent Morello, after all, and Vincent didn't do anything without reason.

"The Catholic Church includes over a billion people. Any move the Church makes is scrutinized by millions, which gives each move outsized import. Such attention is not always wanted. For example, to associate the Church in any way with this neo-fascist group is to provide a spotlight on it and draw attention from around the globe."

"In other words, you don't want to do anything to publicize the Werewolf Group." Harry sighed. "You want me to take action on the Church's behalf."

"Consider this an opportunity."

"Sounds like you want me to figure out what sort of mess your Pope created two thousand years ago. Risk my neck and spare you some unwanted press?" Roberto did not respond. "You can't even tell me what I'm looking for."

Finger drumming again. "I've been told you are quite adept at this type of undertaking."

Harry said nothing, pondering. He understood that the most important part of Roberto's ask remained unsaid. Was it a chance for him to prove himself in the field? Sure. Would it help the Church? Probably, not that he cared. But hanging above all this was how it would reflect on Vincent Morello. Harry jumping in to help the Church on Vincent's behalf? That was priceless.

"Fine."

Roberto opened his mouth to respond. Harry spoke quickly. "On one condition. If I ask you a question, you tell me the truth. Otherwise, the Werewolf Group becomes your problem, not mine, and I'm gone."

"Agreed," Roberto said. "You will have every measure of support I can provide."

Harry nodded. "I need a phone, and I need transportation."

"A vehicle or a plane?"

Roberto, it seemed, had money to spend. "I'll know once I finish my research. Any chance you can get me to a good library?"

"We will be at a most excellent one in a few hours. Perhaps you can rest on the way?"

That's when Harry noticed the city of Florence was now well behind them. He fought the urge to jump from the speeding vehicle. Vincent had said to trust this man. No choice now. "Wake me up when we get there."

Nearly dying made a man tired. Harry leaned into the plush embrace of German leather, closed his eyes, and in what felt like minutes woke to Roberto tapping him on the shoulder. Harry sat up and Roberto inclined his head toward the windshield. "We have a modest collection here. Perhaps it will do?"

Harry blinked sleep from his eyes as the vehicle slowed to a stop. “Whoa. This should work.”

A man walked to the driver’s door. A man with a submachine gun strapped across his chest. The building looming behind the guard was so tall it blocked out the falling sun, with a single spire stretching high above the roof. Roberto had taken him to the very center of Catholic power. Or the rear entrance, at least. “I’ve never seen St. Peter’s Basilica from this side,” Harry said.

“It is quiet here,” Roberto said as they were waved through the gate and their driver pulled around to a pair of smaller doors. Guards stood on either side of the entrance. Both were armed like their colleague outside the walls. “You will have full access to our library for as long as is required.”

Harry got out and followed Roberto through a nondescript exterior door leading to an equally unassuming hallway, which opened into yet another passageway not meant for public viewing. All that changed when Harry went through another set of doors and found himself in a bibliophile’s paradise.

He stepped inside and stopped. Harry craned his neck back, then back some more. Shelving surrounded him on all four sides in a concert-hall-sized room. “This is incredible.”

Roberto guided him to a nearby table. “Ask any employee should you require assistance. I will return in an hour to be sure all is well.” He hesitated. “One other item. The man you heard on the radio in my car.”

“The guy who hates everyone.”

“He hosts the most popular fascist podcast in Europe. Recently he has talked of snakes in great detail. I worry about his message.”

“About snakes.”

"I worry that his words can inspire men to action," Roberto said. "What action, I do not know, but it will not be good."

"Then why don't you have one of your friends in the government arrest him?"

"No one knows who he is," Roberto said. "He wears a mask and disguises his voice while broadcasting. His podcast is called *The Final Stand*, and he claims he is the last bulwark against the decay of the modern world."

"You say he has a big audience."

"Which I'm certain includes the Werewolf Group."

Roberto left, and Harry found himself alone. Except for the half-dozen anonymous men who sat at desks or occasionally got up to walk around. They hardly gave him a look. Harry took his phone out and called his father. "You won't believe where I am right now," he said in a whisper.

"Try me," Fred Fox replied. Harry did. "I did not see that coming."

"I'll let you know what I learn." He pulled Constantine's second sword from the carrying case. Nobody seemed much bothered that he had a weapon with him in the library. "The only lead—"

"One moment." His dad cut him off to hold a muffled conversation. "Sorry, son. I have to go," he said, and abruptly clicked off.

Harry set his phone down on the table. He wasn't the only relic hunter employed by the Morello family, and in the duo of Fred and Harry Fox, there was a clear pecking order.

Harry took the skull drawing from its hidden compartment and laid it on the table. He stared at it, frowning. "What are you trying to say?"

Solving this required thinking like Pope Sylvester or Emperor Constantine. This image carried a meaning not only those two would have known, but one that the Irish pagans would have grasped as well.

For how long he sat there, staring at the skull, Harry couldn't say. He studied it from every angle. "Okay," he whispered to himself. "Let's start at the beginning."

He retrieved one of the available laptops from a man who turned out to be the librarian and searched for the term *skull.*

Nearly ten thousand hits. Refining the search to include the names Constantine and Sylvester returned nothing that caught his eye. He tried again, adding *skull* and *Ireland*. Nothing. Skull and pagan? No dice. He rubbed his chin and stared at the screen. Come on. Think.

A soft orange glow crept into the edge of his vision. Harry looked over to find the librarian standing beside the main entrance, one hand extended. The sun had nearly disappeared outside the large windows lining the library wall, which offered a view of a parking lot and the rear of a security fence, along with the darkening sky. The librarian had turned on lights that encircled the room. Lights that glowed like firelight. A memory came back. "The Irish celebrated Samhain with bonfires." He keyed in *bonfire* along with *skull*. The first return nearly made him shout out loud.

Minutes later Harry had the correct book in hand and was back at the table. He studied the cover and the title, written in Italian, a language he'd spoken since childhood. "*Pagan Rituals of Europe.*" It was a collection of European pagan celebrations, and it included a description of the bonfires of Samhain.

He flipped pages and found hand-drawn illustrations throughout the book, some more detailed than others. He turned over the final page and found it. Harry let out a breath. "No way."

Not merely a section with a skull-and-bonfire reference, but an image nearly identical to the skull in Constantine's sword stared back at him. Except this wasn't a human skull. It was much bigger. "It's a cave."

Harry checked the sword's drawing again. "It's a match." The disconnected lower jaw was an entrance, while the upper portion was a rock formation that resembled a human skull. Where did such a cave exist? In the far northern reaches of ancient Brittania. A land where pagan beliefs had existed over generations.

"Inverness." The corner of his lips turned up. He'd never been to the north of Scotland. He'd need a guide. And he knew the perfect woman for the job.

Chapter 4

Rome, Italy

Broken glass glittered on the streets as flashing police lights whirled. Uniformed officers hung yellow tape, which fluttered in the chill night air. The first news reporter on scene stood beside a bearded man whose eyes were grim behind his wire-rimmed spectacles.

A man sitting in his office miles away muted the television but left the image on-screen. "Excellent." He set the remote down on his desk, then turned toward the man seated across the desk from him. His lips spread to reveal a mouth full of even teeth. "Excellent work." Malvolio Buffon pointed toward the big man sitting in a too-small chair. "Demeter, you have redeemed yourself."

A bandage ran across the side of Demeter's face, covering a cut suffered during his fall from the Ponte Vecchio bridge. Fortunately for Demeter, he'd managed to climb out of the river and avoid any police before they could question him. Malvolio had not been pleased when he learned of his subordinate's failure to bring him the Roman sword. Demeter knew that to displease Malvolio was to invite retribution, so the big man had quietly set a plan into motion to atone for his failure.

“I am glad you approve,” Demeter said. “It did not take much to convince them to attack the mosque.”

In addition to chasing down items valuable to the Werewolf Group, Demeter also worked to further their aims by less obvious means. He cultivated a network of mostly young men, often unemployed, who believed that society had been stacked against them. Well-paying jobs and the security those brought were out of reach. Demeter’s assurances that change was coming if these men would only band together stoked a fire in the recruits, a fire Demeter used to light the path ahead. How best to take back what had been stolen from them? By showing those who didn’t belong that they were not welcome.

“The mosque will not re-open for weeks,” Demeter said. “The firebombs assured it.”

“The sooner it reopens, the sooner we have another target.” Demeter kept quiet. “It shows the invaders they are not welcome,” Malvolio continued. “We will not sit back and do nothing. It is a step forward.” He paused. “A small step. Not the progress we need.”

“I will find a bigger target,” Demeter said.

Malvolio’s chair creaked when he stood. He was of average height, with a slim build, and his longish brown hair was combed straight back so that it reached nearly to his neck. The public had little idea this well-groomed, confident man controlled an effective and insidious neo-fascist group here in Italy. Exactly how Malvolio wanted it. Nothing to identify who they truly were, except for one image.

Malvolio stopped in front of an ancient fireplace and looked at a small, unobtrusive painting hanging above it: an image of a werewolf, the center of their existence. “We have more important matters to handle.”

Demeter gave a questioning look. "What is more important than staying active?" A grimace as his wound protested. "Sir," he finished through gritted teeth.

Malvolio studied the painting. It consisted of four lines, which resembled the letter *Z* turned horizontally, with a single line through the center bisecting the design . A symbol based on medieval European wolf traps, when metal hooks hung from chains were used to capture the animals. Malvolio had changed the original black and white to green and pink, which gave the image a less threatening appearance. Until he told anyone who was curious the meaning behind the colors, that is.

Malvolio turned away from the painting. "We must create the future. Not by desecrating mosques or demonizing false Christians, however." He considered. "Valuable though that may be, our future lies exposing the truth."

Demeter had the good sense to look properly confused. "What truth?"

"Come with me." Malvolio walked past the seated man and opened his office door. "The others are waiting."

Demeter rose and followed him into the hallway. The office complex was housed on the first floor of a two-story building with the main entrance off a small side street. The second floor was unoccupied. Few visitors came through the front entrance; the side entrance was busier. Malvolio knew the men had arrived over the past half-hour while he was meeting with Demeter, and that they had walked in alone.

"Who is waiting?" Demeter asked, finally catching up to Malvolio.

"Our team."

Malvolio walked into the conference room where the eight leaders of his organization had gathered. The men sat at tables facing a podium at the front of the room. They were Malvolio's trusted lieutenants, true believers who made their group's vision come to life. They recruited new followers, and they acted. Their heads turned as the pair walked in.

"Have a seat and listen," Malvolio told Demeter, then strode to the podium. "I have news to share." The men sat in silence. "Last night was a good night," Malvolio said. "Thanks to Demeter here, the heathens in that mosque will look over their shoulders for a long time."

Rough cheers sounded for Demeter, who was looking at Malvolio with something close to suspicion. Demeter followed orders, but he didn't appreciate being left in the dark about this meeting.

Malvolio waited for silence. "Last night was not enough." That got their attention. "Smashing windows at a synagogue or torching a welcome center for refugees is only the start. We can make them fear us, can make the enemies of pure Italians worry for their safety, but that will not change what matters most. All must see that we are a nation under attack. A nation collapsing on itself unless we change the minds of those who have not yet joined us." Another beat passed. "We need a symbol to show the world the truth. That the war rages on. A war against the unrighteous and unholy. A war for Italy. For too long we have allowed the corrupt and weak to lead us to ruin, led by a man in white who claims to speak for all. He lies, and is as corrupt and decayed as those he warns against."

"The Church," one man called out.

"Yes." Malvolio pointed east, toward Vatican City, and his voice rose. "The Catholic Church. We will show the hypocrisy they traffic in, the lies on which they stand. How will we do this? By proving they are criminals who do whatever is required to keep themselves in power and who destroy anyone standing in their way.

"Our new symbol comes from an agreement made two thousand years ago. They could never have foreseen this, but an ancient Roman tyrant and a bygone pope will give us our chance to show the world the Catholic Church is a place of evil, hiding behind a mask of forgiveness and sin."

Malvolio reached under the lectern and removed a manila folder. "Last month I obtained a book. A copy of a Roman-era text by a Roman emperor. It proves what I say—that an agreement was made and the Church is built on lies."

Malvolio pointed at Demeter. "The sword you lost held the answer. I need that sword." He glared at Demeter. "Except it is at the bottom of the Arno River, lost forever, so we have a new task. We can still find what we need, and this will lead us to what will disgrace the Church." Malvolio lifted a hand. "What I am about to share cannot be repeated." The men leaned closer. "This sword leads to a treasure of gold and jewels. Riches that are a symbol to the world of a corrupt church ready to be discarded."

He brandished the folder again like a weapon, showing the righteous anger of one who had not been told the truth. Malvolio didn't have the answers, but he had faith, and faith could topple anything. "This book shows that a pope conspired to slaughter an entire people. Not the heathen Muslims, but the innocents."

The folder slapped onto the podium. "I have an assignment for each of you. Demeter will take two of you with him to recover the sword. The rest of you will prepare to let the world know the Church's true nature. The end of this evil Church will follow." Malvolio clenched his fist. "To achieve this, we must find one man. His name is Harry Fox. He knows the truth about this sword. We will find him, and he will tell us."

Malvolio told the men their orders would be delivered soon, then dismissed them. Demeter and his two chosen associates followed Malvolio back to his office, where Malvolio paused beneath the green-and-pink symbol of the werewolf. Green for rebirth, as Italy would be reborn with only true Italians. Pink for the blood needed to achieve this rebirth. The blood needed to revitalize this true nation. Malvolio had an American patriot to thank for the inspiration.

The tree of liberty must be refreshed from time to time with the blood of patriots and tyrants.

Thomas Jefferson could not have been more correct.

Chapter 5

Inverness, Scottish Highlands

"It's a small world, Mr. Fox."

Harry Fox offered what he hoped was a disarming grin. "Maybe it's fate."

Lauren Brosnan came at him before he could do the same, wrapping her arms around him and squeezing as tightly as she could. Harry caught the scent of freshly washed hair. Other passengers slid around the embracing couple before she let go. Harry still had the grin on his face. "Thanks for flying in from Dublin."

"You think I would miss a chance for another adventure?"

A few short months earlier, Harry and Lauren had nearly been killed a few times following a path across Ireland to chase four supposedly mythical Irish treasures. Which had turned out to not be so mythical after all. When he'd last seen her, Harry almost asked when they might meet again. But he hadn't, and she hadn't asked either. In the months since that day, however, Lauren Brosnan was never far from his thoughts. That's why the skull drawing had been a gift from the gods. It brought Lauren back.

"Ready to go?" she asked.

Lauren was not one to wait around. Harry hefted his travel bag on one shoulder and walked beside her to the car rental area, where in short order she was behind the wheel with Harry beside her as Inverness Airport faded in the car's rearview mirror and harvested fields surrounded them. The dark and choppy waters of Moray Firth to the west suggested summer had retired from the Scottish Highlands, pushed away by chill autumn winds.

Lauren turned onto a two-lane road with a field on one side and tall trees with leaves turned to vibrant fall colors on the other. Harry snuck a look at her, then decided not to hide it. "How's life in Dublin these days?"

When they'd first met, Lauren worked for a fundraising organization called the Irish Heritage Society, a group dedicated to preserving Irish sites of cultural importance. A select few within the group had an additional focus. Including Lauren.

"Still working to fulfill my destiny."

"Which destiny is that, Your Hi—"

"Don't say it." Her voice was steel. "Don't." Harry lifted his hands in surrender as Lauren continued in a lighter tone. "My worst enemy now isn't an invading army. It's paperwork. Endless paperwork." Lines creased her forehead as she smoothly maneuvered around a sharp bend. "I can't believe how many applications are involved in creating a new national exhibit. Simply getting permission to *apply* for building permits is a fiasco."

Harry spotted a stone mansion that had likely been there when Leif Erikson reached Newfoundland. "Doesn't your government want to display its cultural treasures? Why so much red tape?"

"It almost seems that those in power want to keep these recovered artifacts hidden for as long as possible."

The Four Treasures of the Tuatha Dé Danaan were thought to be mythical objects from ancient pagan stories. The truth was they were real. Harry and Lauren had recovered them, only to discover the truth could prove inconvenient to some people. Influential people.

Lauren waved a hand to indicate the topic was closed. "Enough about my problems." Her bright hair flashed in the afternoon sun. "You have more surprises than any man I know. First, Irish treasures. Now, a Roman sword."

"Thanks." He coughed until his cheeks weren't so warm. "Lucky for me I have the best guide in Ireland."

"Flattery will get you everywhere." She laughed. "I've researched the Clava Cairns since we spoke. My guess matches yours; we should focus on the Skull Cairn."

The Clava Cairns were burial chambers situated not twenty minutes outside of Inverness. Dating to the Bronze Age, they included dozens of ancient burial sites marked by different types of cairns, which were human-made piles or collections of stones. Some were tall, wide single stones, while others were stone mounds, some with conical raised peaks. Among the different cairns placed over hundreds of years, one had caught Harry's eye during his research. In fact, it wasn't a true cairn. It was a cave.

Lauren seemed to read his mind. "The Skull Cairn is a cave that happens to be near the cairns."

"A cave that looks like a skull," Harry said. "What can you tell me about it?"

"One, it has no stone markers. Two, there's no one buried inside."

"You sure about that?"

"I am," Lauren said. "As are a hundred other people far more qualified to speak on the matter. The Skull Cairn is visually distinctive, but beyond simple evidence of human use, by which I mean fires and food waste, there's nothing inside."

"Bears?"

"Wild bears were hunted to extinction long ago."

"By fires, you mean ceremonial fires."

"Large ceremonial fires," Lauren said. "Massive blazes, the sort lit during Samhain celebrations."

"Intended to light the way for the dead."

"Skull Cairn was perhaps the most haunted site in their ancient world—the portal through which souls passed to return to their homes and be welcomed by the living. People even set places at their tables for expected dead loved ones. The fires symbolized both the passing of the old and the rebirth of the new."

"Marking the end of summer and the coming of a long winter."

"With the warmth of spring to follow," Lauren said. "A worship of the natural order. Hardly unique to Ireland. Although Samhain also ties back to your favorite topic. Irish myth."

He knew this, but he let her tell him, because that way she kept talking. "Irish myth and treasure," he said. "My two favorite topics."

"The sword matters now. The sword and the message still matter. You should know history doesn't give up its prizes easily."

"I'm listening."

"Your sword has a name. The Sword of Fionn mac Cumhaill."

"In the myth, Fionn slew the fire-breathing being Aillen, who burned down Tara every year. I read the story. I also know Samhain hasn't faded away."

"Because Samhain is still celebrated by different faiths today?" Lauren asked. "Even you Americans have a holiday tied to it. We can talk more about that later."

"Why later?" Harry asked.

"Because we're here."

They turned off the highway onto a winding, two-lane paved road that came to a narrow bridge with room for only one vehicle. Another turn put them on an even tighter road hemmed in by low-slung stone walls on either side. Harry didn't have time to get his bearings before Lauren turned into a small parking lot and pulled to a stop.

He got out and looked around. "Good. We're the only ones here."

"The cairns are over there." She waited for him to grab a pack from the car, then walked through a short row of trees to a grassy field with taller trees on all sides. Mounds of stones dotted an open area that was the size of several football fields. There were several larger individual stones scattered in the field that Harry recognized as individual grave markers. The markers and stone piles had been laid over thousands of years by various peoples, their stories lost to history, though their mark remained.

"Skull Cairn is on the other side of those trees." Lauren pointed past the largest circular mound of stones. "There are enough leaves left to give us some privacy."

"I'll get the sword." They'd wanted to survey the area before carrying the sword through the burial grounds. Harry loped back to the car and returned to find Lauren already nearing the tree line shielding Skull Cairn. Fall leaves blocked the late-morning clouds momentarily as they passed wide tree trunks and walked up a gravel path. The hillside leveled off above them to show nothing but gray skies overhead, so when Harry reached the end of the path he had no idea what to expect. The sight of what waited stopped him cold. "Wow."

They crested the lip of the plateau and stared into the empty eyes of a giant.

"Incredible how the cave entrance resembles a human skull," Lauren said. She did not step any closer. "And creepy."

The cave opening was more wide than tall, perhaps ten feet high. What made it creepy were the trio of circular openings above the cave entrance. A smaller opening centered a few feet above the ground-level entrance resembled a nasal cavity, while the two larger openings several feet above it looked like two empty eye sockets. A rounded hilltop completed the eerie effect. It looked like a skull.

"Those openings are natural formations," Lauren said. "The cave roof is at the same level as the eye sockets. There's nothing unusual about this at all."

"Other than it could be a portal to the world of the dead."

"Other than that." Lauren seemed to steel herself. "Come on."

Suitably impressed, Harry followed her to the cave entrance before halting. "You've been inside here before?" he asked.

"Yes. It's not terribly interesting. Here, take this." She handed him a flashlight before turning her own on. "The first cave inventories found animal bones with knife markings on them."

"Showing they were butchered or cut during consumption."

"Which also proved humans used this as a gathering location or for shelter. People could stand on the plateau and light massive fires for Samhain. The evidence from oral and written accounts of the area shows this was a central point for Irish Samhain activity."

"*The* central point." Harry looked at the sword in his hand. "Bonfires to hold back the darkness of the coming winter and to light the way for souls of the departed to return. What does that have to do with this sword, though, and are there graves inside the cave?" Harry asked.

"There are cairns farther back." By which she meant piles of stones and single stone markers.

"Have they been excavated?"

Her eyes went wide. "No. We do not desecrate these graves."

"Why not?" He gestured down the hillside. "Those were."

"These are different." Her tone brooked no dissent. "These cairns are protected by the Irish government, as they have been for nearly a century."

"I don't see the government anywhere."

She ignored him as her flashlight beam lit a wide black scorch mark on the floor. "When we adopted our current Constitution in 1937 there were provisions added to preserve certain sites." She indicated the cave around them. "Including this cairn."

Harry's nerves lit up just a bit. "No one knows what's under any of the cairns."

"The remains of our ancestors." She gave him a quizzical look.

"Maybe that's not all," Harry said. "I'm not saying we desecrate your ancestors' final resting places. I'm saying we explore all possible solutions to this mystery. Then put things back exactly as we found them."

"We could be arrested."

"Don't worry." He winked. "We won't be."

She laughed. "Fine. But we do it with respect."

He hefted the sword, putting away his light so he could hold it with two hands. "Shine your light over here," he said.

"What is it?"

Harry didn't respond. Metal flashed as he moved the sword this way and that until the point faced down and the pommel faced up. "Nothing." He grabbed the flashlight from his belt and aimed it into the cave. "Let's go."

What little light came from outside faded immediately. Their combined flashlight beams pushed away the cave's total darkness as they walked. The cave was deep. "It must go back a hundred feet," Harry said. He turned and looked up. The empty eye sockets and nose behind them made it seem like the skull looked in both directions—inside the cave and out—never losing sight of the intruders. He turned around and did not look back again.

"Here's the first cairn." Lauren indicated a circular grouping of stones perhaps ten feet in diameter. None of the stones was bigger than a dinner plate.

Harry leaned over and inspected each visible stone in turn. "You don't think these have been moved?"

"I don't believe they've been moved for ten centuries. Look for gaps between the stones."

Harry did. "There aren't any." Debris caked what had once been gaps between stones. He poked some of it with the sword to find it had hardened to natural concrete. "More good news."

"If there's anything hidden inside," Lauren said. "It should still be there."

"You should be a relic hunter." He stood as she rolled her eyes. "Are there other cairns?"

"This one doesn't interest you?"

"Not enough."

"Why not?"

"I'll tell you later." Harry led the way deeper into the cave. A standing stone came into view. Set vertically into the ground, it rose like a tombstone to waist height. He inspected its front and back. "No marking or writings," Harry said. "This isn't it."

"You sound certain."

He didn't tell her he had little idea what to look for. He'd know it when he saw it. "The cave ends back here. I see one more stone."

"It's the final one," Lauren said as they approached the standing stone. "Burial back here was limited to a select few, perhaps leaders or the ruling elite."

"It's big," Harry said. This vertical stone reached to his shoulders; it was thick at the base and as wide as him at the top. "Someone went to a lot of effort to get this up here."

Harry's light brought the rough stone alive. Chips of reflective minerals sparked like gems in the dark rock. He leaned the sword against the stone before running his palm over the surface and then reaching to the back. His hand stopped on the far side of the rock. *I knew it.*

"Come over here." She moved so fast he nearly lost his balance. "Give me your hand," he said. She did, and he ran her fingers over the rear surface. "It's mostly smooth." He lowered her hand until it was nearly at floor level. "Except here. Feel that?"

"It feels like an engraving." She moved around to the rear, shining her flashlight down. "I can barely see it."

Harry picked up the sword and walked around to stand beside her, leaning the sword against the rear of the standing stone. "Does the mark look familiar?"

She angled her light. "Is it an inverted *V*? I can make out two lines that come together at the top. Wait, there's a horizontal line between the two vertical ones."

"The letter *A*."

She looked up. "What does it mean?"

Harry put his fingers on the sword as he spoke. "Look above the *A*. See?"

She had to kneel. "There's a wavy line. I missed it. Sort of like a cloud, perhaps? A cloud with spikes on it. Or a row of connected *Vs* one after another that encircle the upper half of the letter."

"I think it looks like a fire burning with the letter *A* inside it," Harry said.

"That's a great descript—Hold on." Her gaze was hot on him. "How did you know that?"

Harry responded by moving his hand so the sword he touched, still point-down in the dirt, moved to show the pommel's bottom. "The same engraving is at the bottom of this sword."

Lauren lifted the sword and held it close to her face. She looked at the stone, then the sword again. "They're identical." She shoved the sword toward him.

Harry grinned. "Before you ask, I'm not certain what it means." He lifted a finger. "But I have an idea. Constantine and Sylvester gave this sword to the Irish. A gift with a message. This symbol carried meaning for the Irish. Which deity from Irish mythology begins with an *A*?"

"Aed," she said. "The god of the underworld."

"And why the fire?"

"Because of Samhain," Lauren said. "The reason we came here."

"Agreed. So, what should we do next?"

Lauren looked at the standing stone. She looked at the sword, then to the ground. Her response was low and deliberate. "We find Aed."

"By digging." Harry put his arms out. "This stone is a marker. Not for a grave. For where we *dig*."

Lauren reached her hand to the top of the standing stone. "We need—what's this?" She rose up on her toes and moved her hand along the top of the stone. "There's a hole here."

"Of course there's a depression in it. Stones aren't usually flat."

"It's not a natural indentation." She was able to put her entire hand into the stone. "It's a big hole someone cut in here. Look." He grumbled and leaned over. He studied the stone. He stopped grumbling. Lauren's soft words made his spine go cold. "I think the sword will fit into this hole."

Could it? Harry lifted the sword, put its point just above the hole, and lowered it in.

"It fits." Lauren helped him push it, but suddenly grabbed his hand as the sword was still moving. "What if there's a trap?"

Harry let go of the sword. Thankfully, Lauren held on. He looked around, checking the floor, the ceiling, the cave walls. Nothing stood out. "You push it in. I'll stand back."

"Very funny."

"You think I'm joking?" The look she gave him was enough. "I'm joking." He took hold of the sword handle and pushed Lauren away. "Get back. If this goes south, call my dad."

"I like him better than you anyway."

Harry jammed the sword down, his arm shuddering as it stuck fast. He leaned back but held on, his face turned away with one eye clenched shut.

"It didn't work." Lauren stepped closer to Harry. "The sword is the key. It fits inside," she said. "That can't be coincidence."

Harry didn't respond. He grabbed the sword's cross guard and twisted. The sword spun, rock grated on rock, and with a final shove it turned in an entire circle before stopping with an audible *click*.

The cave shook. Harry's vision blurred as dust fell from above. He didn't run. He couldn't. "Look." Harry pointed at the rear wall. A section of it had fallen open. Darkness waited beyond.

Neither Harry nor Lauren moved. "I knew it," Harry said. "Constantine and Sylvester built this."

"In a cairn," Lauren said. "Without anyone knowing."

Harry lifted his light to get a better look at the tunnel. "The floor's dirt. I don't see any footprints."

"No one ever found the passage," Lauren said.

"Let's find out why not. The answer's in there."

Harry moved to the opening. Two people could walk through it abreast, and he could scrape his fingers across the top of the passage if he reached for it. "It's big enough for a cart to fit in. With a horse, too." He tried to picture what might have come this way so long ago. And why create this hidden space?

Lauren moved to the edge of the door and pointed at the rock. "Tool marks. This tunnel is man-made."

"I don't think it's deep." The doorway appeared solid, as did the interior walls he could see from where he stood. "I don't see any traps."

"As in hidden spears or tripwires? Holes for burning oil?"

"For starters." All manner of deadly devices had protected the Irish treasures they had pursued months earlier.

"We won't find anything standing here." Harry hefted the sword as though a dragon might be ahead. "Stay close. Don't touch anything."

He ignored Lauren's glare as he stepped through the door.

Chapter 6

"Look at that."

Harry stuck the sword out to halt Lauren's progress. He nearly impaled her. "Sorry," he said. "Look."

She was too absorbed with what he pointed at to berate him. "It's identical."

A human skull image on one wall of the passage. Identical in shape and design to the image on the scroll inside the sword, except this skull was as large as a man. "We're in the right place."

"Is it a warning to keep out?" Lauren asked. "Skulls aren't usually drawn on welcome mats."

He waved her concern away. "Keep moving."

The smooth dirt softened his footsteps as they moved deeper into the cave, the floor sloping downward. "The passage is getting smaller," Lauren said. She looked left, then right, and stepped closer to Harry.

"We have plenty of room," Harry said as he took another step. He stopped when Lauren spoke.

"What is that?" she asked.

"What we came for."

The tunnel ended some twenty feet ahead. Not in a sheer wall, but at the mouth of a wider chamber. Harry forced himself to take it slow until he stood at the end of the narrow tunnel and the beginning of something new.

The walls opened on either side to a low-roofed circular chamber roughly forty feet in diameter with bare walls. The floor, however, was not bare. "Do you recognize the design?" Harry asked, pointing down at a series of concentric circles carved into the floor. He knelt and peered at the cut stone. "It looks like a maze."

"There's an unlit torch," Lauren said, shining her flashlight beam up. It settled on a torch sconce attached to the wall beside them. Sticks bundled with string waited to be lit.

"There's a string beneath the torch," he said. His light followed what resembled twisted rope from where it was attached to the torch and ran to the floor. "It ends inside part of the floor design," Harry said. "Not on top of it. Inside the floor." The stubble on his chin rustled as he rubbed it. "It looks like a fuse. Maybe I need to light the torch, then use it on the fuse."

"Which will do what?"

"I'll tell you in a second." He handed the sword to Lauren, sent a silent thanks to his dad for teaching him to always carry a lighter, then pulled it from his pocket and flicked the wheel. Sparks flashed, a flame came to life, and seconds later the ancient rushes on the wall were ablaze. They both stepped back and watched.

Flames moved quickly down the braided fuse until they hit the floor and the show really got started. Fire burst to life inside part of the floor carvings, burning a path that zigged and zagged around the room toward the rear wall before turning back on itself and returning to the beginning in a mirror image. Smoke filled the air and Constantine's intent became clear.

"It's a path," Harry said. "The flames show a path through the floor maze." Flames burned to knee height with enough room for one person to walk through without getting scorched. "We should follow that path through the maze to the rear wall."

The rear wall that came alive as he watched. Once the flames had burned for several beats, a square section of the rear wall fell back. The piece thumped down and dust billowed. Harry narrowed his gaze to see through the smoky dust. "Latin writing," Harry said.

"*How to vanquish the wulver?*" Harry translated the Latin words to English as he read the message aloud. "It's a question about something called a *wulver*. I've never seen that word in my life."

"Yes, you have. The modern equivalent, at least. The wulver is a Scottish myth about a creature with the body of a man and the head of a wolf. Contrary to the modern depiction of an aggressive creature that appears during a full moon—the werewolf—the wulver always looks the same and spends most of his time fishing. He's friendly, giving his catch to the hungry and the poor, and he aids lost or injured travelers in the woods where he lives."

"Sounds nothing like our werewolf."

"Wulvers only injure humans in self-defense," Lauren said.

"So a wulver is not a werewolf. It's not hostile, it gives to the less fortunate, and it lives in the woods. Sounds like Robin Hood to me."

"The Robin Hood legend didn't exist for a thousand years after Constantine's time," Lauren said. She waved the smoke away from her face. "But the stories do share one common thread. Both shared their spoils with the poor. Also, Robin Hood stole treasure, and Scottish wulvers were supposed to be able to lead worthy men to treasure in the ruins."

Harry waved a hand at the far wall. "Think those count as ruins?"

"Perhaps, though it would seem no one ever found a wulver to lead them to the treasure."

"Or there weren't any worthy men in Scotland." He did not see her fist coming until it slammed into his arm. "I'm joking," Harry said. "I'm sure all the worthy people were women."

That got a grin out of her. "Do you plan on taking this burning path or not?"

"I'm getting to it," he said. "The question has me stuck. These wulvers don't sound mean. Why would you want to vanquish a wulver?"

"Some versions of the legend portray them as terrifying beasts." Lauren shrugged. "There are many variations."

"Maybe I'll find out more at the other end of this path." Harry handed over his flashlight. "There's plenty of light," he said. "But not plenty of breathable air. Let's move."

She agreed. He hefted the sword, took in a lungful of oily air, and stepped onto the chamber floor directly between two burning lines. Harry continued taking cautious steps until he reached a ninety-degree turn in the path and could walk closer to the rear wall. Another sharp turn took him parallel, the flames forcing him to walk in a zigzag pattern until he made it to a spot directly in front of the rear wall. A circular wall of fire penned him in. "I see two drawings on the floor," Harry called out. "They're in color."

"Are they paintings?"

"No. Images engraved on the floor with some type of coating. One looks like a dagger. The other is a fire. They're within a circle of fire on a part of the floor that's raised several inches."

Lauren wasn't concerned with that. "What colors are they?"

"A silver dagger and a red fire." Dark shadows flitting about the room made it hard to see clearly, so he stepped up onto the raised area of the floor and moved forward until he was directly in front of the two images.

The floor rattled and rocks cracked as loud as gunshots in the chamber. He shuddered, arms flying out as the ground beneath his feet moved. It fell, dropping down and taking Harry with it until it was level with the rest of the floor.

"Did the floor move?" Lauren asked. Harry said it had. "I saw you drop down," she continued. "That circular part must be a trigger of some kind."

"Yeah, but a trigger to what?"

"I suggest you don't find out."

I don't plan on it. He pushed the concerns away. Want to get out of here in one piece? Figure out what these pictures mean. Black smoke curled around him and sweat dripped as he studied the drawings. Why paint these images? Harry looked to the wall, then back to the images. The sword in his hand reflected flashes of red light. "It's a choice," he shouted. "And the sword is the key."

The sword flashed as he lifted it overhead. Recognition dawned on Lauren's face. "You use the sword as a key for the keyhole beneath an image."

"Except which image do I choose?"

It was a test. Which would vanquish the wulver? Acrid smoke burned his throat with each breath. Sweat dripped from his chin and his eyes stung. He snapped his fingers. "Silver! Just like werewolves. I bet silver kills them. The fire is for Samhain and lighting the path for spirits, not for vanquishing wulvers."

He hefted the sword with both hands, flipped it so the tip pointed down and aimed for the dagger hole.

Lauren shouted from behind. "Wait! Two choices means one is wrong. If the door shuts behind us, we're trapped in here."

Where they would starve to death, unless fire and smoke did the job first. Harry shook his head. *I'm sure it's the silver dagger. Silver is how you get rid of a wulver.*

He hesitated. Fire surrounded him. Why so much fire?

Ragged coughs wracked a scorched throat. The sword came down, banged into place, and Harry twisted it.

Beneath the image of a fire.

Stone shuddered and the floor rose. Harry turned to run. The fires waned. *Phew. Silver daggers didn't kill werewolves. Silver bullets did.*

The flames in front of him faded before burning down to nothing. Light still flickered in the chamber, and Harry turned to find two parallel lines burning in front of the question on the wall. They led directly to the carved Latin words like runway landing lights.

"Part of the wall came loose." Harry took one tentative step forward, then moved to the rear wall and knelt to inspect the baseball-sized rock. "This fell out of the wall." He looked up. A new, smaller hole was right in front of his face. Harry probed inside the hole with his finger. A shiny object reflected orange and black as he reached in. "It's a dagger. A dagger with jewels on it." Harry removed a weapon of breathtaking beauty. Garnets and sapphires lay along the pommel, the garnets casting a reddish-orange light while the sapphires were so dark as to appear black. Harry gently turned it over. "There's a message here on the blade."

"We can read it outside," Lauren said. "This place is dangerous."

Lauren was not joking. Harry turned to find her walking away and not looking back. He set off after her. Back and forth they went, following the same path. Once outside the chamber entrance Lauren stopped, taking deep breaths of the fresh air. She stuck her hand out for the dagger.

"Check the blade," he said as he handed it over.

Lauren didn't acknowledge him. Her gaze was on the dagger, which she held up toward the gray sky, trying to catch what scant light made it through the clouds. Harry stepped toward her, drawn by the sudden intensity, and stumbled. He looked down at the ground. A broken branch lay by his foot, the exposed wood bright, not weathered, its splintered pieces sharp. As though it had just been snapped. When did that happen?

"Another Irish legend."

He looked up and went to her side. "Show me."

She didn't hand the dagger over, instead holding it with one hand and pointing at the row of letters engraved into the blade. "It's incredible. This dagger is the only Roman artifact I've ever seen with ties to Irish mythology."

"What about the first sword that led us here?"

"Okay, the second." Her enthusiasm was undimmed. "This shows a Roman emperor and a pope who understood the importance of Irish mythology, and they used it to their advantage." The enthusiasm darkened. "But how?"

"That's what we're going to find out." Harry read the Latin silently. "This first part doesn't make any sense."

"Because you don't know of Stingy Jack."

Not another Irish myth. "Enlighten me."

Lauren extended the dagger to him, then thought better of it and pulled the weapon back before he could take it. "Pay attention. Then you'll be able to understand the message." Harry crossed his arms, using one hand to make a *get on with it* motion. "Stingy Jack was an Irishman. Deceitful, manipulative, and he liked to drink. A lot. Stingy Jack was such an awful man that even Satan heard of his misdeeds and decided to come to Earth to see if anyone could truly be so awful."

"Sounds like Satan would approve of the guy."

"He did," Lauren said. "Satan found Jack, who realized his time was up and a fiery eternity awaited him. Jack asked Satan for one last drink before their trip to Hell. Satan took Jack to a pub where Jack asked Satan to pay for the drink. Satan doesn't carry money, but Jack had a solution. He told Satan to turn himself into a coin so Jack could pay the bartender, and then Satan could change back when the bartender wasn't looking. Satan admired Jack's devious nature, so he went along with it."

Harry was intrigued. "Bad move."

"Very bad. Jack put Satan—now a coin—into his pocket." One corner of Lauren's lip turned up. "The pocket where Jack carried his crucifix. It prevented Satan from changing back, so with Satan at his mercy, Jack struck a deal. He'd let Satan turn himself back if he spared Jack's soul for another ten years."

"Satan didn't have much choice."

"He didn't, so he agreed. Ten years later he came for Jack again."

"I'm betting that didn't work out either."

"Jack pulled another trick. He asked Satan for a last apple. Satan agreed and began climbing a tree to pick the apple. Jack surrounded the base of the tree with crucifixes, trapping Satan once again. Stuck on the tree, Satan had to agree to Jack's demand that the devil *never* come for his soul."

"Satan should have hired the guy."

"Eventually Jack died and went to heaven. God told Jack he couldn't come in due to his wicked ways, so Jack went to Hell and begged to be let in. Satan reminded Jack of his promise to never take Jack's soul, which meant Jack couldn't enter Hell either."

"Where did that leave him?"

"The devil gave him an ember to light his way as he roamed the world between good and evil. An ember he carried inside a hollowed-out turnip."

"A turnip?"

Lauren lifted an eyebrow. "You don't know it, but you know this tale as well."

"I've never heard about an empty turnip and a burning ember before."

"The legend changed over time. The ember became a candle, and the turnip became—"

"—a pumpkin." Harry shook his head as it hit him. "Halloween pumpkins started with a myth about a turnip?" Lauren nodded. "That's wild," Harry said. "But how does this legend help me understand this?" He pointed to the phrase engraved on the dagger and read it aloud. "*The mountain of the witch is accessed only with Stingy Jack.*"

Lauren's hair flitted as the wind picked up. "I'm not sure yet," she said.

Harry pointed at the dagger. "Lucky for you I think I do know where to find it. Come on."

His boots thumped as they moved down the hillside. Lauren trailed behind, asking where they were going and getting no response. Down the hill, through the trees, and then they crossed the field and cairns before Harry stopped beside their vehicle in the parking lot. Tiny stones almost as fine as sand had been laid down to create the parking area. Harry's boots left faint impressions in the damp ground where he walked. One hand on the door, he hesitated, looking back across the parking area toward the road.

Lauren jumped in the car. Her door shut, she leaned over to look out the window at him. "What is it?" she asked.

Harry didn't respond. He knelt close to the ground and narrowed his gaze. Were those lines on the ground? Sure enough, two parallel lines ran back to the road and led to the exit. As though a two-wheeled vehicle had parked far back and pulled out the same way. "See this?" Harry asked.

Lauren stepped back out. "Do I see what?" Harry indicated the faint line. "You mean the tread marks in the ground? Those are tire tracks," Lauren said. "Either a motorcycle or one side of a car that had the other tires on the grass."

Harry had not considered that option. "They weren't here when we arrived."

"Are you certain?"

He was not. He didn't say it, though she read it on his face. "I didn't see them," he said evasively.

"I don't see anyone around." She waved her hand to encompass the empty area. "It could be from yesterday and we missed it. Or perhaps someone came while we were in the cave, then left. It's a public area. Anyone can come and go here."

"My gut says it's not good."

She lifted a shoulder. "We'll stay alert."

He grumbled, not too loudly, and took one final look around. "I guess you're right."

She hopped back in the car, and he joined her. "We're getting closer," she said. "Now tell me where you think we can find the answer about a witch's mountain and Stingy Jack."

That pushed the concern away. "You'll see soon enough," he said as she put the car in gear and hit the gas. "And I promise, it's the sort of place you'll love."

Chapter 7

Inverness

"You're joking," Lauren said. "You cannot take that inside."

Harry had just parked outside the Inverness Public Library a moment ago. Lauren frowned when he slid the dagger found in Skull Cairn into his waistband and got out of the car. Harry leaned back inside, both hands on the car roof. "It's not very big."

"It's basically a Jim Bowie hunting knife."

"Excellent American cultural reference," he said. "But this is smaller. And what if I need it for my research?" He lifted the hem of his shirt and replaced it over the dagger handle. "Nobody can see it. No one will know it's there."

Lauren shook her head. "You were correct, I do love libraries. And a library is no place for weapons." She didn't press the matter further before getting out and heading down the sidewalk.

In the wrong direction. "The entrance is this way," Harry said.

She held up her phone. "There's an issue at the Irish Heritage Society. You get a head start on unraveling the next step. I'll find you as soon as I'm done."

How could she think of work at a time like this? The answers were practically at hand. Whatever they needed had to be inside.

"I won't take long." She winked. "You don't need me. This is what you do."

She turned and walked away, phone pressed to her ear, unaware of the effect her words had. He'd rather she stayed here, solving this alongside him. But the warmth of her praise would not fade quickly. He turned and headed into the library at a fast clip. This *is* what I do.

Six columns fronted the library entrance, three on either side, the twenty-foot pillars of granite giving it a solemnity he believed all libraries deserved. The door opened to a wide central space with bookshelves running along every wall and an open second level that somehow managed to contain even more shelves than the first level. Polished wood floors reflected soft lighting, giving the interior an almost underground feel, as though it were insulated from the chaos of the outside world. A circular staircase led to the second level. Harry walked past it and headed to a computer terminal.

Harry opened a browser to the library's catalogue, put his hands on the keyboard, and hesitated. What am I searching for? A tie between witches, a mountain, and Stingy Jack. Not much to go on. His lips pursed. Harry typed the dagger's phrase into the search bar. *The mountain of the witch is accessed only with Stingy Jack.*

Over a hundred results flashed on the screen. Books on mythology, articles about the origin of witches, geography textbooks, and accounts of the Salem Witch Trials. Too vague. He tried *mountain of the witch*. That kicked back—oh. *That's interesting*. The Loughcrew Cairns in County Meath had existed for thousands of years, as had so many cairns across Ireland. What did distinguish them was another name they were known by. *Sliabh na Callaighe* was a moniker given to the area to describe the hilly terrain. The translation? Irish for *Moun-*

tain of the Witch. According to legend, the hills had formed when a witch attempted to perform the feat of strength required to prove she could rule over all of Ireland. Her feat required leaping from hilltop to hilltop weighed down by massive stones in her apron. During this endeavor she had dropped some of the stones, which formed the cairns that stood today. To top it off, she didn't land the final jump that would have made her ruler of all Ireland; instead, she broke her neck in a fall and ending up buried beneath the very stones she had carried.

"This could be it." Harry clicked on the next link about this legend. More of the same, and despite checking the top ten search returns, he couldn't find anything linking the Loughcrew Cairns to Stingy Jack. He marked a volume to pull from the shelves and tried a new search combining *mountain*, *witch* and *Irish mythology*.

"Slievenamon Mountain." He murmured the name quietly to himself. "Never heard of it." It had returned on several of the top results, a mountain in County Tipperary, Ireland, some ten hours southwest of Inverness. Whatever Constantine and Sylvester had done, the answers appeared to be found in Ireland. Harry scribbled down the location of another book on the new mountain and headed up the winding staircase to the upper level, where he located the first book on Loughcrew. He moved between the stacks, looking for the second book on Slievenamon Mountain. A noise made him turn to catch a glimpse of a patron walking briskly along beside the railing that kept people from falling to the ground level. The patron never glanced Harry's way.

Gray skies were visible through the windows on the rear wall, and Harry paused to look outside at the half-empty parking lot. A streetlight flickered off and on in the dim afternoon light. The shelf he sought was beside him. Harry reached out, one finger running across the call numbers until he found the book and pulled it from the shelf.

The floor creaked beside him. A man now stood in the walkway, looking at Harry. A man about Harry's height, slim of build, hard of face.

"Hello," Harry said. No response. Harry tucked the book under his arm and moved to pass the man. The man did not move. "Excuse me."

"Harry Fox."

The sound of his name made him jump. "What did you find in that mountain?" the man asked.

It took Harry a moment. "Sorry, pal. You have the wrong guy. My name's Joey." The lie rolled smoothly off his tongue.

"You are Harry Fox." The man spoke in English, but his Italian accent was impossible to miss. "You and a woman were at the mountain today. You went inside." The man shifted so he had one foot slightly in front of the other. His hands were at his sides. "What did you find?"

The man sounded calm, his tone assured. Bookshelves stood ten feet high on either side of Harry, with windows to his back. Harry could try to shove him aside and run, but all this guy needed to do was take a step back and mirror Harry's movements in either direction to keep him penned in. Harry could yell, though who knew what the guy might do if that happened. The man wasn't any bigger than Harry and he didn't seem to have much backing him up beyond a scowl and a hard voice. It could be a fair fight. Too bad Harry didn't believe in fighting fair.

"Listen." Harry shook his head. "I have no idea what you're talking about. Now, move aside."

The man did not move. "Stop lying or this will not go easy for you."

Harry reached under his jacket and pulled the dagger out. "I asked nicely." Harry held the blade by his waist. "Now I'm telling you. Get out of my way."

The man laughed. "You will need more than that."

The man stepped back and reached around to the back of his waist. One second Harry had the guy at a disadvantage. The next, Harry was staring down the barrel of a pistol. *Oops.*

The man waved the gun. "What did you find?"

Harry stared at the gun. His dagger suddenly looked much smaller, and after a moment of feeling foolish he put it back in his waistband. The man with the gun didn't seem to notice the dagger was a relic. Harry lifted a hand, the one holding two books. "I'll show you." He indicated the books in his hand. "The answer is in here."

The man craned his neck to read the titles on the books' spines, and didn't flinch when Harry held out one of the books. Harry watched the gunman's eyes as the man backed up a step. "Hold still," the man ordered.

Harry held the book out with his left hand, keeping the other book in his right, tucking it down to hold it like a frisbee. "Don't shoot," Harry said. "Take the book. Look inside the front cover."

The gunman put a hand out to take the book. Harry leaned closer, tensing his right arm, holding it tight against his body. He kept the proffered book in his left hand, holding it out wide, away from his body. The gunman's fingers touched the book. *Now.*

Harry whipped his right arm out, spinning the other book from under his arm on a direct line for the gunman's face at the same time as he slapped the book in his left hand down onto the pistol.

The spinning book smacked the man's nose, and cartilage cracked as the gunman recoiled. Harry's second book missed. The gunman still held his weapon. Harry jumped at the man, sliding past the pistol in case it fired as he threw a punch at the man's wounded nose.

The guy twisted to let Harry's fist slip past his face, blood from his broken nose flicking onto Harry's knuckles before Harry stumbled ahead. The force behind his errant punch sent Harry flying at the railing. He bounced off the metal rails before a strong hand grabbed his shirt and spun him around, and Harry found himself nose-to-barrel with the pistol once more.

The gunman grimaced. "You are stealing our treasure," he said. "Tell me what you found. Last chance."

The man stepped back before Harry could respond. A half-step, far enough to be out of harm's way, close enough that Harry had no escape. He glanced over a shoulder to the ground level, and the empty table directly below him. "Fine." Harry lifted a hand. "You need this."

He reached into his waistband and removed the dagger. "The message is on here," Harry said. The gunman's eyes widened. "On the blade."

Harry slowly turned the dagger over, pulling it slightly closer to his chest as he did. He waggled the dagger like bait on a hook. "This is what we found."

The man reached out for it. Harry put his weight on his front foot, his eyes on the gunman's face, his throat dry. Wait for it. *Now.*

The gunman's fingers grazed the dagger's handle. Harry let the knife drop as he grabbed the man's hand and pulled him forward, turning aside as the pistol fired with the noise of a cannon inside the library. The bullet skimmed past, how close Harry couldn't say, but he kept pulling and used his other arm to grab the man's back and propel him up and over the railing. Legs flipped skyward, a shout joined the gunshot's thunder, and the man went headfirst over the railing. Harry leaned over as wood splintered and a grisly crash sounded from below. The first screams came an instant after the table split in half. The gunman lay between the two broken sides, one arm at an unnatural angle, one leg not much better.

Panicked screaming bounced off the walls from the downstairs patrons. *Time to go.* Harry scooped up the two books and the dagger he had held and ran for the staircase, leading the charge of several people in a circling race to the ground before going to kneel beside the fallen shooter. Harry shouted orders as several other people looked on, telling them to call an ambulance, digging in the guy's pockets all the while. His fingers closed on a cell phone, which he jammed in his own pocket before jumping up and running outside at the tail end of the rush.

Panicked patrons ran down the sidewalk or sprinted across the street to where onlookers stood huddled with hands on their mouths or phones pressed to their ears. Harry darted between them, the books under one arm and the dagger hidden under his shirt, headed to where he'd last seen Lauren.

Lauren must have been walking to meet Harry when the chaos broke out. She was the only one fighting to get through the crowd moving *toward* the library. Harry made a straight line for her and spoke quickly. "Follow me." He held up the two books. "I borrowed these." The first sirens sounded in the distance. He accelerated, Lauren keeping pace until they were several blocks away from the library and the crowd gathered on the street. Harry led her around a corner of a parking garage and stopped. "Hold these." He pushed the two books toward her.

"A book about Irish mountains?" Lauren checked the second book. "And Irish cairns? Why more cairns?"

"One is about the Loughcrew Cairns," Harry said. "The other is about Slievenamon Mountain. I'm not sure which is the answer."

He shoved a hand into his pocket and his fingers closed on the pilfered cell phone. "I have to check this."

She gasped, suddenly noticing the blood on both his hands and the phone. "What happened in there?"

"A guy stuck a gun in my face." Harry swiped on the phone screen to unlock it, sending a silent thanks to the cell phone gods when it opened without requiring a passcode.

"Whose phone is that?"

"The gunman's."

"Did he *shoot* you?"

"He missed." Harry frowned. "No calls on it. Probably a burner." He opened the messages. "Check this out." He turned the phone screen so Lauren could see the photo.

"That's you," she said.

"Yep." More scrolling, though the phone had precious little else to reveal. "Only one text chain. Seems like updates." He read one of the messages aloud. "'Located them at the cairns. He's not alone.'"

"They're talking about us."

"Told you those tire tracks at the cairns were trouble."

Harry read out another one. "'At Inverness Library. Going inside.'" The next message brought goosebumps to his arm. "'*D* is waiting.'"

"'Dee'?"

"The letter, not a name. No idea who it is." Harry shoved the phone in his pocket and ducked behind the concrete garage wall, motioning to her to follow. "Come on." He nudged her out of sight of the library. "We're headed back to Ireland."

Lauren walked beside him as a bus rumbled past. "Where in Ireland?"

"We'll figure that out at the airport. The answer is in one of these books."

Chapter 8

Rome

A line of police in riot gear stood silently behind bulletproof shields. The demonstration had not gotten out of hand. So they waited.

The permit for this demonstration—properly filed and approved—identified the group as the Catholic Alliance for Peace. They were gathered to publicly advocate for peace in the Gaza Strip. It had all come about after the Israeli government razed a few tin shacks in Gaza, tin shacks that turned out to have Gazans inside them when a bulldozer ran them over.

Not that Malvolio Buffon gave a tinker's damn about Gazans or their shanties. He cared about opportunity, and this peaceful protest against the Church's silence was very much one. He stood among the protestors, wearing a hat and sunglasses that hid his face. Hundreds of protestors were on hand for this gathering, which was outside a synagogue. An equal number of counterdemonstrators stood across the road, on the opposite sidewalk, to oppose the protestors.

Malvolio also had men embedded within the counterdemonstrators. A few even wore traditional Jewish attire. His men didn't stand out for any reason. They carried the tools of their trade out of sight: stun guns, flares and smoke bombs, which, Malvolio reasoned, should be enough to turn the typical chanting into a much more destructive experience. An experience that changed minds.

Malvolio stood a block away from the protestors, near the curious onlookers and a handful of news crews, their cameras rolling. Exactly what he needed. Malvolio pulled out his phone and sent a one-word message. *Ready.*

His men quietly put their hands in their pockets, opened the zippers on their jackets and wrapped their fingers around flash-bangs and smoke grenades. He had assigned twenty men to each side, in plain sight among the protestors and counterprotestors, more than enough to push the whole event into chaos. Malvolio had even facilitated the rallies, greasing the right palms on the public authority boards to have permits issued and any police presence reduced. Nobody knew it was him, of course.

The brisk morning breeze never reached Malvolio's bones. Nothing could chill him right now. Small steps like what was about to happen would change the world. Malvolio narrowed his eyes and scanned the crowd. Any moment now.

Chants sounded. Signs waved. Fists shook.

No smoke filled the air, no bangs pierced the noise, no shouts of panic rang out. Malvolio's jaw tightened. There should have been smoke bombs going off, flares burning and flash-bangs firing. He'd sent the message. Malvolio grabbed his phone.

Except he hadn't. He shook his phone and tapped the blue arrow to fire the brief message out into the world once more. That's when it hit him. *I have gloves on.* He shook his head at the stupidity of it, removed a glove, and tapped the screen again.

Malvolio barely got his phone back in his pocket before the first smoke bomb went off. One thick stream of white smoke, quickly followed by another and another, and things got rolling. Flashes of light turned the smoke into a pulsating curtain, each flash punctuated by concussive bangs. People screamed and the first scuffles broke out in the thickening haze. His men had been chosen for their brawn instead of their brains. Each of the muscle-bound hooligans he'd placed in the crowds began shoving indiscriminately, knocking peaceful protestors into the police lines before ducking out of sight. The riot police needed little encouragement to push back, trying in vain to stop the fighting.

Brawls erupted, police sirens blared, punches and kicks and broken noses sprang up at every turn before the final piece of chaos arrived. Several of his men had firecrackers that sounded like gunshots, and when those went off, the police charged through the terrified protestors shouting for people to get down. Malvolio stood far off, at the perimeter of the disaster, enjoying the scene. His men scattered, dropping leaflets that would later tie this debacle to ultra-conservative Christian groups who before today had shown no appetite for violence. The damage would be done even if they claimed no involvement.

Time to go. The evening news would be filled with images of anger toward a church that had seemingly lost control and could no longer be trusted. Those images would be the catalyst for people on the edge, people who might find refuge in the welcoming, righteous arms of the Werewolf Group. Malvolio turned and walked away from the wonderful debacle, headed for headquarters. More people would come to him in the days ahead, eager to embrace the ideals he held so dear. Today would strengthen their cause, bringing them one step closer to crushing the failed institution built on Saint Peter's rock.

Back at his office, Malvolio checked his watch; he had slightly more than thirty minutes before Demeter would check in. Enough time to stoke the recruitment fires once more. He went to a nondescript door in his office, opening it to reveal a small closet, its only contents a row of jackets hanging on a single rail. Rain jackets, winter coats, even a reflective work-zone jacket in blaze orange. He pushed them to one side and flicked a light switch on the inside of the doorframe.

Click. The rear wall fell back to reveal a large opening. Malvolio stepped past the coats and closed the closet door behind him. A soft light filled the space until he stepped through the opening and hit another light switch that illuminated a recording studio.

Two hooks were off to the side. Each held a single item. Malvolio took the black judge's robe off one hook and slipped into the familiar fabric, zipping the front closed to cover his body up to his neck. The other item hanging on the wall required two hands to lift. Its strap went around the back of his head and the familiar mask settled into place. Malvolio turned on the recording equipment, monitors and the computer on a table coming to life. None of the millions who listened to his podcast knew the man behind the robe and mask, not with his voice electronically altered for the recorded broadcast of *The Final Stand*. All they could see was a red-tinged skeleton mask speaking the truth.

Malvolio had chosen his disguise based on a story he enjoyed. Edgar Allan Poe's *The Masque of the Red Death.* The story about how death stood close at all times. People needed to know this. People like the Jews and Muslims, the blacks and Asians, all of whom were conspiring to hold back the one pure race. That—the apocalyptic danger his people faced—was Malvolio's message, his way to shepherd his followers back to their rightful place as leaders of a changed world.

He sat and began recording. Thirty minutes later the week's message was complete. It would go out in the morning to over a million followers, downloaded around the world. The mask and robe went back on their hooks, and Malvolio exited the hidden recording chamber and put the curtain of jackets back in place.

He closed the closet as a knock sounded on his office door. "Come in." The door opened and Demeter walked in, followed by a subordinate named Len. Both had been in the crowds. Len had a puffy eye and a bruise on his chin. Blood stained the collar of his shirt. "What do you have for me?" Malvolio inclined his head toward Len. "Any injuries or arrests?"

Len knew better than to acknowledge the damage to his own face. "No injuries of note. One of our men was detained. He will not talk."

Malvolio turned to Demeter. "See to it he has legal counsel," Malvolio said. "And the demonstrations?"

"More than fifty arrests," Demeter replied. "Ambulances, two burning vehicles, and there isn't a window on the church that's intact. More news crews were arriving when I left."

"And the literature distribution?"

"I stuffed handfuls of the pamphlets into the shirts of a few people." Demeter offered a grin devoid of humor. "They weren't in any condition to take them out."

Which meant Demeter had pounded a handful of unfortunate protestors senseless before putting paperwork on them to suggest that they were members of ultra-Christian factions and were responsible for the violence. News agencies could now report on possible motives. Nobody would pay attention to these groups' claims of innocence. They'd remember the news reports and the images of unrest.

Malvolio didn't show any satisfaction, however. "What about our social media efforts?"

“Running at full speed,” Demeter said. “Posts going up for the next two hours. We will flood the airwaves with our truth.”

Malvolio could churn out a nonstop stream of falsehoods to confuse the public. He’d build the message that people tied to the Church were to blame for this violence. That it was a lie didn’t matter. The narrative would stick, and more people would look at the Church as a relic of the past, a group of old men holding others down. All part of his campaign to show the discontented and angry people of Italy that action was needed. And who better to lead the charge than him?

Malvolio motioned with his hand for the two men to be seated at a table across from his desk, then brought his laptop over and joined them. He touched a key on the keyboard and a large monitor came to life on the wall. “Momentum is on our side,” he said, turning toward the screen. “Public perception of the Church is low already.”

“People hate the Church,” Demeter said.

“Not yet, but we’ll get there.” Malvolio pulled up a national news page. “Look,” he said. “It’s the top news story.” A headline shouting about unrest at the protest took center stage.

“People are unhappy,” Malvolio went on. “That’s the wedge we use to drive them away from the Church. It is a void we will fill.” His tone darkened. “Unless you can’t take care of one man.”

Demeter growled. “We are handling him.”

Malvolio raised an eyebrow. “We?”

“*I* am handling him.”

“Yet I understand he’s in the wind.”

“A temporary setback.”

Malvolio’s face pinched. “You followed him from the Clava Cairns to Inverness Library. You had him cornered. How did he get away?” Demeter started to growl and opened his mouth to speak. Malvolio waved the explanation away. He already knew the story, as he had been waiting outside for an ambush that had never occurred. Their man inside the library—armed, mind you—had been outclassed by the man from New York. The ensuing debacle had concluded with their man under arrest in a Scottish hospital and Harry Fox in the wind. All Malvolio had gained from the mess were the titles of a pair of books Harry had been carrying and his man's claim that Harry had been armed with a dagger. A dagger that told where Harry would go next. In short, he had nothing.

"You failed," Malvolio said. "You have no idea what that may cost us."

Demeter wisely declined to point out he hadn't been in the library at all. "You asked for more information on Harry Fox," Demeter said. "He may be more of a problem than we realized."

Malvolio's head snapped around. "How?"

"He has ties to organized crime in New York."

Malvolio almost laughed. "Organized crime?" An arm went out to encompass the ancient city around them. "Half the men here in Rome have *ties* to Cosa Nostra. It means nothing. Besides, what sort of name is Fox?" Not a good Italian name, that was for certain.

"His father works for Vincent Morello."

Malvolio's hand froze halfway to the keyboard. "You're certain?" Demeter said he was. "Is his father Italian?" Demeter said he was not. "Then how close can he be with Vincent?"

"Part of his inner circle."

Malvolio stood straight. "Impossible."

"Rumor says it involves a blood debt."

Malvolio turned to look Demeter full in the face. "Vincent Morello owes Fox's father his life?"

Demeter shrugged. "Supposedly."

Vincent Morello was New York's *capo di capi*, the boss of bosses. As old-school as they came. Whatever the elder Fox had done, it was big. An American as part of Vincent Morello's inner circle shouldn't be possible.

Malvolio shoved the sizable concern aside. "Find Harry Fox, learn what he knows, and make sure he disappears." Malvolio's eyes narrowed. "If you don't, I will."

Demeter understood the implication. A second-in-command who couldn't be counted on was a man whose time had ended. "It needs to be quiet," Demeter said. "We can't alert Vincent Morello."

"Which is why you will find Harry Fox quietly, get rid of him, and continue to follow the path from Constantine."

"To find proof of an agreement between a Roman tyrant and a pope," Demeter said. "Which is important."

"It is the key to everything. It proves the Church is evil. The modern term for what they orchestrated is ethnic cleansing."

Malvolio recounted details laid out in the ancient manuscript. They told the story of how an emperor and a pope had conspired to trick the pagans into believing a chance existed for peace. They had given them a gift to lure them onto a false trail, with terrible consequences to follow. The pagan religion would suffer a devastating blow, leaving the Christian faith to continue accumulating believers and marching to global dominance.

"Their pope will be exposed for the hypocrite he was," Malvolio finished. "Selling salvation while demanding payment."

"Religions have done this forever," Demeter pointed out.

"Only because no one could stop them," Malvolio said. "They couldn't stop Constantine destroying Irish beliefs and giving the people no choice but to follow his god. That's changed. Now, I can stop them."

"How?" Demeter asked.

Malvolio pulled out his phone and held it up. "I told everyone. On our podcast." The cover art for *The Final Stand* was on the screen. A red mask of death. Only Demeter and a few trusted associates knew Malvolio to be the man behind the red mask. "Did you listen to the podcast today?"

"Yes," Demeter said. "You talked about snakes a lot."

"Symbolism." The phone went into a pocket. "Our followers need a sign. A sign that they must act."

Understanding dawned briefly on Demeter's face. "Leave the Church."

"And join us. All they need is a push to join a movement that will reshape the world. We will show them our path is righteous."

"That's what you said in the podcast about the snakes," Demeter replied. "That a righteous serpent from the past will arrive as a sign."

"It will be the final piece that shows the world who is righteous."

The understanding dimmed. "A snake?"

"A statue from antiquity," Malvolio said. "A statue we will use to change everything." His voice lowered. "A statue you let slip through your grasp."

Demeter had the good sense to keep quiet as Malvolio crossed his arms. "We will find Harry Fox, who has followed the trail laid out by Constantine and Sylvester. He will find the statue. We will use him to get to the statue, and then we'll show the world how corrupt their church is. The disillusioned will flock to us. And that will be enough."

Demeter summoned a resolve Malvolio hadn't expected. "We are not certain where he is."

"I have many friends, including some in the Church."

"Inside the enemy?"

"I obtained the book about Constantine and Sylvester from an archivist in the Vatican. He gave me a copy."

"Why would he do that?"

"To save his family," Malvolio said. "People are easy to control. Find what they love and threaten it. They listen quickly after that."

Demeter nodded in approval. "Can this man in the Church help find Harry Fox?"

"He will help us find the American," Malvolio said. "Or his family will be sorry."

Chapter 9

Inverness, Scotland

Harry and Lauren sat in the bar at Inverness Airport, discussing their next moves. Harry believed their options were either Loughcrew Cairns, known as *the mountain of the witch*, or Slievenamon Mountain, which seemed more like a long shot. Harry had explained his thinking to her as they sipped their drinks, but she'd barely listened.

"You know better than to blindly trust history books," she had replied.

He failed to muster a response beyond a confused "What?"

She tapped the books on her lap. "Come on, Harry. You should know history is an educated guess at best. Forget about it being written by the victors. Often what we read is based on memories of stories and old tales."

"What does that have to do with caves and mountains? Those aren't stories. They're real."

She gave an exaggerated sigh. "The *geographic features* are real. The *names* may not be. People give different names to places all the time. We are looking for a mountain tied to a witch in some way. Maybe everyone understood what mountain that was two thousand years ago. Do you think it's so clear-cut that what you found referenced today is what Constantine meant when he wrote this?"

Harry wasn't letting her steamroll him. "I sure hope so. It could be."

"Hope is a terrible plan." A few moments passed in silence as he sipped his beer. Lauren took a sip of her own drink and scrutinized one of the books again. Suddenly she smacked a palm flat on the bar, making Harry jump. "I *knew* it. Look at this." Lauren spun the book around for him to see. "I was right."

"Right?"

She flipped the book back around. "I was right about the clue meaning something we didn't expect." She put a finger on the page and read aloud. "I found it in a footnote."

Harry narrowed his eyes at the line of text. "It's a note about the origin of the word *witch.*"

"And it tells us where to look next." Her words came quickly, tumbling out one after the other. "The origins of *witch* are uncertain, but one theory is that the word is actually a mistranslation of another word. You need to know the background to understand why."

Harry nodded, then pulled up the airline's website on his phone. "I need to buy our tickets to Dublin. Give me the short version."

"The root word of *witch* probably meant a person with wisdom or knowledge. However, in a widely distributed version of the Bible, the Hebrew word for *witch* described a poisoner."

"So the context of the word *witch* as detailed in the best-selling book of all time makes it seem that witches poison people." Harry shrugged. "What does that mean for us now?"

Lauren flipped the book around again to show a centuries-old illustration of a mountain. "This mountain was known in ancient times as a place to avoid because poisonous plants grew there. Local people called it *poison mountain*. Any guesses as to what that colloquial name became over time, after the Bible with mistranslation came to be?"

Harry snapped his fingers. "Witch mountain."

"Exactly." Lauren closed the book. "Buy us two tickets to Dublin, and rent a car there. We're driving to Tipperary County."

The flight to Dublin went smoothly, and as Harry drove their rental car south to County Tipperary, he and Lauren continued to ponder the mystery of the message on the dagger Harry had recovered in Skull Cairn. He needn't have worried. Lauren had unraveled it completely by the time they arrived. A short walk from the parking lot brought them face to cliffside with the mountain Lauren deemed to be the answer. "Slievenamon Mountain," she said. "This is where Constantine wants us to go."

"I like Witch Mountain better."

"Why?"

In response, Harry pointed at the rising slope in front of them. Over a thousand feet of granite and brown grass interspersed with shrubbery, vertical rockfaces and what appeared to be the occasional wild game trail. A thin layer of cloud hugged the uppermost portions. "The word *spooky* comes to mind," Harry said. "I like this place. Plus, it keeps with the whole Halloween angle Constantine appears to have unintentionally laid out. Witches, werewolves, this Stingy Jack guy. It's hard to miss the connection to Halloween."

"You would have a point if the concept of Halloween as we understand it today had existed in his time. But it didn't. Today's Halloween is somewhat like America. A big, mixed-up, wonderful cauldron of various parts stirred together that creates something new." A gust of wind kicked up and snaked down Harry's collar. Lauren waited for it to pass. Her tone was much darker when she continued. "Though this modern-day tradition is rooted in an act we don't fully understand."

“Why would an emperor and a pope go to this much trouble for a statue?”

“I hope the answer is up there.” She indicated the mountain peak far above. “Burial cairns are on top of the mountain. Several hiking trails lead there.”

“Which worries me.”

“Worries you?”

“Anything we’re looking for may already have been discovered.” Harry lifted a shoulder. “Or it could still be hidden because we’ll be the first to understand their true intention.”

On the flight and drive there they had discussed areas of interest connected to Slievenamon Mountain. The cairns stood out as an obvious destination, though another historical aspect of the mountain had grabbed Harry’s attention. A trio of standing stones at different levels on the mountainside. Not a path, as they were not erected in any discernable pattern and stood far away from each other. Still, their existence piqued his interest. What had been engraved on each, though, had really caught his eye.

“The ancient Irish thought the cairns were portals to the underworld,” Harry said. “It’s an obvious target.” He crossed his arms. “Too obvious. I like another pagan feature.”

“The three standing stones.”

He nodded. The three standing stones were well-documented. Each stood roughly the height of a man. Latin letters adorned each stone, along with symbols. As far as anyone could determine these were grave markers for once-important Irishmen who had been long forgotten. The symbols seemed religious in nature, or at least were suspected to be. But a smaller detail drew Harry’s attention.

“One of them is made from foreign stone,” he said.

Two of the standing stones were carved from material native to this area, likely from this very mountain. Which made sense given each stone weighed north of two thousand pounds. The third stone was different. His research had revealed the material for it had been quarried in Italy. It was assumed the marble had been repurposed by the local Irish from some Roman object. A statue, most likely. The symbolism of turning a prized Roman statue into a marker was too much for the ancient Irish to ignore.

"I think the marble was brought here with intent," Harry said. "Used by the Romans to leave a marker from Emperor Constantine."

Lauren nodded thoughtfully. "An interesting theory." She looked toward a path that wound upward across rough ground, strewn with loose stone and patches of coarse grass that clutched the earth like old scars. "Say you're correct and the third stone sends a message. What could the letters and symbols mean?"

A softball question and she knew it. "It has two letters and one image. *X*, *S* and what resembles an inverted cross."

"Likely the initials of the person buried beneath the stone, along with their clan crest."

"What if those aren't initials?" Harry asked. "What if the letters are a message?"

"Saying what?"

"That Constantine and Sylvester are coming for the Irish. Coming for their beliefs. The Irish had offered Rome and the Vatican a symbol of peace. I don't think the empire or the Church had any interest in returning that offer. I think the *X* meant an ending, that something was over. The *S* tells us what it was."

Lauren's breath turned to faint, silvery mist as she spoke. "That's a stretch. No scholar has ever suggested as much." She lifted a hand to stay his argument. "No other scholar knew what we know. I understand. What do the letters mean?"

"The end of Samhain."

"That would be incredible," Lauren finally said. "Without more evidence I can't offer an intelligent response." A fair reply. "What about the clan crest?"

Harry reached into his shirt and removed the dagger. "It's not a crest. It's a dagger."

Her eyebrows went up. Harry inclined his head toward the low, gray sky above the mountaintop. "Let's go find out. Come on."

Signs marked trailheads leading up the mountain. With no trees to speak of, Harry could see the first half of their route as it moved up the mountainside, a moderately challenging back-and-forth hike before the trail veered to one side and disappeared over a ridge. The standing stone Harry wanted lay beyond that, a hike of about a half-hour or so if they climbed without stopping. Harry put his head down and began walking, Lauren at his side.

It took fifteen minutes. The idea that Constantine's trail could end shortly ahead made Harry move with purpose. The wind whistled around them, dry grass waving on either side of the path, an eerie soundtrack to their course.

They crested the ridge and walked into a wall of stiff wind. "Legend says the wind is the cries of fallen warriors," Lauren said.

"We're not here to bother them," he said. His eyes went left and right. "In case they're asking."

The gray sky lowered toward them with each step. Distant flashes told of a storm on the horizon, though no thunder sounded and the bad weather looked as though it would keep its distance. Beyond the ridge their path settled into a narrow valley, wisps of fog hanging above the grasses, the ghostly tendrils parting as they approached, disappearing when Harry reached out a hand as though to push them aside. The hairs on his neck rose. He looked back to find the fog had returned and closed in, as though they'd never passed through.

"We're here," Lauren said.,

The standing stone waited a hundred feet ahead, resting on a small plateau. The path led up a small rise to the flat ground. Harry jogged the last few feet up the slope so he could examine the entire stone. "I didn't know it was sheltered," he said.

A wall of granite lay behind the standing stone, a sort of backstop for protection that gave it the aura of a place for devotion. He could see why some believed this standing stone to be a memorial. He could also see proof his theory held water. "There's plenty of stone right here to quarry," Harry said. "The fact they brought in marble is telling in itself. It's telling us to pay attention."

The white marble of the stone gleamed against the granite wall backdrop. Harry stood before it and pointed at the first letter. "The *X* and the *S* are aligned," Harry said. "Like writing."

"Are you fitting facts to support your theory or the other way round?"

"The facts do fit my theory," he snapped.

"What about the clan crest?"

The recovered weapon came out. "This dagger is similar to the stone engraving." He held it next to the stone. "The proportions are the same, and the handle looks like this one."

"Along with a million other small knives," Lauren said. "It's a stretch."

She might be right. That didn't matter. "I'm telling you, they match. I can feel it."

"Fine." Her hands found her hips as a gust of wind sent her hair jumping. "Say you're correct. What does it mean?"

He had no answer. A lone bird flew overhead. Far below, distant cows the size of ants milled about in fields. And as Harry Fox stood on the side of this Irish mountain surrounded by the spirits of an ancient myth, he knew he was right. He just knew it.

Harry walked close to the stone, put one hand on his chin, and studied it. Say this dagger was the one on the stone, and the two letters were a message saying the Irish holiday was doomed. There had to be a way to prove it. A way to access this witch mountain by knowing the legend of Stingy Jack. Harry rubbed his chin. *Access.*

He walked around to the rear of the standing stone and found nothing but solid marble. He came back to the front and put one hand on top of the stone, pushing gently. Of course, the stone didn't budge. His fingers brushed against something.

Harry stood on his toes and looked down at the stone from the top. A rough gouge on top of the stone had caught his fingers. An imperfection, perhaps. Harry stepped back, his mind racing as he moved the dagger from hand to hand. The answer lay in front of him. Same as it had done in front of the Irish pagans. He just had to see it. Two letters, a dagger below and between them, the point aimed down.

"Oops."

The dagger slipped from his grasp. Harry danced back an instant before the blade plunged into the ground where his foot had been an instant earlier. It stuck, buried halfway to the handle. Harry bent over and pulled it loose.

"I have no interest in carrying you down this mountain," Lauren said. She stuck her hand out. "Give it to me."

He barely heard her. "Access," he said. He looked at the image of the dagger. Carved directly below the letters, right in the middle. With the point down.

"What?"

He turned to face her. "The message told us how to *access* this mountain. What does that mean?"

"I thought you knew the answer."

"I didn't." He lifted the dagger. "But I might now. How do you access something?" The dagger waggled. "With a *key.*"

He turned, stood on his toes, raised the dagger over his head, took aim, and stabbed down at the standing stone. The blade slammed into the hole you could only see if you were looking down on the stone from above. It went in all the way to the hilt until the blade had disappeared and the entire dagger stuck fast.

Nothing happened. No shaking ground, rumbling stone, or ancient gods appearing. Harry wasn't sure what he expected, but nothing was not it.

"It actually fits?" Lauren seemed more surprised than intrigued. "You could have broken the blade." She nudged beside him and stood as high as she could to look at the dagger handle. "That could have turned into a disaster."

Turn. It hit him. This dagger wasn't only a weapon. It was the key to moving ahead. What did you do with a key? "Turn it." Harry grabbed the dagger's guard, one hand on either side. You turn a key. So he turned it. Hard.

The dagger spun so fast he fell forward and banged his face off the marble, shouting a hearty curse as the blank granite wall behind the stone rumbled open. A section of it rotated on itself to reveal an opening into the hillside.

The rumbling ended. Silence filled the vacuum. Until Harry spoke.

Harry turned to her and winked. "Told you that was a dagger."

Chapter 10

County Tipperary, Ireland

Lauren ran to the opening and held a flashlight out. "There are stairs."

Harry managed to push through the shock that rocked through him and pull his own light out, aiming it into the darkness of the staircase cut into the mountainside. "They built a false entrance over the cave entrance," Harry said. "A darn good one."

Lauren gestured toward the steps. "Mind if I lead the way?"

"A thank you would be nice." Harry waited. "Fine," he said. "You lead the way. Clear out any traps along the way."

"You know Romans often launched surprise attacks from the rear."

She left him with that questionable bit of knowledge and entered the cave, pausing at the top of the stairs to inspect them for danger, which gave Harry a chance to catch up. "You made that up," he said.

"I did."

He ignored her grin and aimed his light down the stairs. A short set of stairs. "It's barely ten feet down," Harry said. "And it looks like we didn't bring the right gear."

Their flashlight beams reflected off a pool of water, the edge of it just beyond the lip of the lowest step. The dry stone walls on either side of the stairs were close enough together that Harry could stick his arms out as he descended and touch both sides on the way down. He knelt at the edge of the top step and inspected the stones for danger. "Looks safe," Harry said.

"Then you go first."

Harry believed in himself, but that didn't make him reckless. He grabbed a loose stone by the cave wall and tossed it down the stairs. The rock bounced on several steps before hitting the ground below and hopping into the water. Nothing.

"Told you." Harry took a tentative step onto the first one, then the second, moving with confidence by the third step as he marched to the bottom, Lauren joining him to stand at the water's edge. They both stood still.

Harry had never seen anything like it. Square pieces of stone dotted the water, each side a foot long, seemingly floating on the surface in rows. The stones rose only a few millimeters above the surface, so faint they could have been a mirage on the black water.

Harry aimed his light across the pool. "They're steps," Harry said and pointed ahead. "The passage ends there. Look at the back wall."

The water stretched twenty feet ahead. Beyond that, dry ground, and the passage's rear wall. Perhaps ten feet of dry stone floor lay beyond the far edge of the water. "There are carvings on the rear wall," Harry said. "I can't make them out from here."

Three niches had been cut from the rear wall and what looked like a stone carving of a plant sat inside each recessed opening. There was writing on the wall directly above the center opening.

"I'm not certain," Lauren said. "First, we need to worry about this."

Her light moved from the back wall to the left wall of the cave, no more than ten feet away. "Latin writing," he said. Harry moved to stand in front of that wall before reading the Latin aloud in English. "*Only by following the path closest to Donn may you cross.*"

"Donn." Lauren snapped her fingers. "God of the underworld in Irish pagan beliefs."

A sharp whistling sounded as the wind kicked up behind them. "Doesn't sound like the kind of guy I want to meet."

"Donn dwells in the house of the dead, the place where souls gather after they leave the earth."

"Any idea what path you take to get there?"

"According to legend, souls could return from the underworld to visit their loved ones on one day of the year."

"Samhain."

"Yes. But the dead had to follow a specific path. The route from the underworld to the world of the living was called the *low road.*"

Great. Their success depended on Lauren's memory and a fuzzy interpretation of an ancient story. "Fine," Harry said. "We take the low road."

"Which path is the low road?" Lauren asked. "Straight across? A zigzag route of back and forth?"

Harry paused. "Where's low on a map?"

"South?"

"That's what I'd say. A practical interpretation. It makes sense." He said it mostly to convince himself. "We use the stones on the left. That's the path closest to Donn."

"Care to tell me why?"

Harry pointed ahead. "That's west." He pointed to the right. "That's north. That's east," he said with a nod over his shoulder.

"Which makes the stones on the left south. Lowest means closest to the underworld. The answer is tricky because it's simple."

Lauren pointed at the water. "Maybe we should check to see how deep it is. Then you don't have to worry so much about the proper stones." Harry declined to touch the water. "Fine," Lauren said. "I'll do it."

He stuck an arm out to prevent her from moving. "My gut says that's a bad idea."

She didn't argue as he walked to stand at the water's edge. The south-most three rows of stone squares stretched across the pool, each square seeming to float on the water, though when he knelt he could make out more stone beneath the waterline. The squares were actually columns, stretching down who knew how far. He looked left, then right.

A series of holes ran along the wall on either side. Small and round, about the size of baseballs, they were barely visible.

"Do you see these holes?" he called out.

Lauren came to kneel beside him. "I suspect those are pipes," she said. "To maintain the water level. Rainwater flows into the pool from the mountain to keep the water at a certain level, and the pipes allow excess water to flow out."

"I just hope spears don't shoot out of them," Harry said. He pushed aside the unwelcome memory of nearly being impaled in a cave near the Uragh Circle with Lauren at his side not long ago. "You might want to get back." He stood.

Lauren stood too, then took a step back. "I'm staying. Grab my hand if the stone collapses."

He did not tell her the odds of her holding him were quite small. Harry steeled himself, lifted a foot, and stepped onto the first stone of the left row with the commitment of a man who couldn't afford to doubt.

The stone held. It took a second for Harry's full-body shiver to disappear.

Water rippled around him as he crossed the five steps. The far side came quickly, both of his boots dripping water as he took the last step and stood on the strip of dry ground. He could now see what Constantine and Sylvester had left for him. Three square openings cut into the wall at chest height, perhaps two feet on each side and a foot deep. Inside each opening was a terracotta jar.

"They're plants," he called back to Lauren. That's what he'd thought from across the water, but in truth he hadn't expected to be correct. He checked the floor, found no trip wires or obvious false spots that could set off a disaster, then walked to stand in front of the center opening. A medium-sized terracotta pumpkin sat inside. A pumpkin with a hole on the top of it. Harry leaned over, angled his light, and looked down into the hole. A braid of fabric that appeared to be coated with a tar-like substance sat in the middle of the pumpkin's interior.

Harry looked to the left opening. It held a squash, or perhaps a gourd. He couldn't say. The right opening? A potato. Each was hollow, like the pumpkin. Harry twisted to look back at Lauren. "You're not going to believe this."

She kept silent while he recited the three garden vegetables. "What about the message on the wall," she said. "What does it say?"

Harry turned back, looked up at the words and translated them aloud. "*Retrieve the soul cake by using the light of Stingy Jack.*" The Irish legend had returned. "Stingy Jack is back," Harry said. "There aren't any cakes here that I can see."

Lauren's flashlight reflected off the water as she swept it back and forth across the area where Harry stood. "There's nothing else?" she asked.

"Nothing. What kind of light did Stingy Jack have, and what's a soul cake?"

"Are you sure you don't see anything else? It would look like a small biscuit."

"I don't see any biscuits here." He glared as best he could across the water. "Why are you talking about biscuits?"

"That's what a soul cake looks like." She finally put her light down. "Do you know the story?"

"Give me the short version."

"Soul cakes were given to children who knocked on a person's door and promised to pray for their departed loved ones. The exchange is tied to the Christian Church's concept of purgatory."

"Like Stingy Jack wandering the earth forever?"

"Sort of. The Christian Church declared that one of the only ways to help a person's soul escape purgatory and ascend to heaven was through prayer." Her tone changed. "Or offering."

"Buying their way into heaven."

"Which the poor couldn't afford," Lauren said. "Children jumped in and offered prayers for the departed to help them get to heaven."

"And they received soul cakes for their prayers," Harry said. "I'm guessing these soul cakes were treats?"

"You should know exactly what they are."

"I've never heard of soul cakes before."

"No, but you're familiar with the tradition. You've done it yourself. I'm certain." He threw an arm up and glowered at her. "You've done it," Lauren continued. "Except you didn't get soul cakes, and you certainly didn't offer prayers."

"What are you talking about? I'm trying to stay alive over here. Out with it."

His flashlight beam made her teeth sparkle when she replied. "Knocking on doors and asking for treats. Does it ring a bell?"

A connection struck him. "Hang on. This sounds like trick-or-treating?"

"It should, because it is. Modern trick-or-treating started with soul cakes."

"What is it with all the Halloween vibes?"

"I think we'll find it's because much of what we do is built on what has come before."

That part he understood. "Constantine and Sylvester also had another goal. A goal the Irish pagans wouldn't like."

"That's putting it mildly." She aimed her beam behind him. "You need to locate a soul cake."

"My guess is Stingy Jack's story will show me the way. But Jack didn't have a pumpkin. Or a potato." He moved to the small root vegetable and peered at it. "At least I think this is a potato."

"He used a rutabaga to light his way," Lauren said. "Hollowed out, and with a candle inside."

Harry had never seen a rutabaga in his life. "You mean those things that look like turnips?"

"They look like rutabagas."

"Assume I have no idea what that means."

She let out an exasperated sigh. "Yes, they resemble a turnip. But what does that have to do with the next step in this search?"

Next step. "A step I find by using the light of Stingy Jack." Harry looked inside the terracotta pumpkin and it hit him. "These are wicks." He repeated it louder so Lauren could hear from the cheap seats. "The fabric inside here is a wick. It's coated in tar. Anyone who made it in here would need to have a torch to see."

"Meaning they would have access to a flame," Lauren concluded. "Is there a wick inside the rutabaga?" Harry said there was. "Then light it."

"Might want to stand back," Harry said as he pulled a Zippo from his pocket. The lucky green shamrock on it offered faint reassurance as he touched the flame to the wick. Sparks flew. He ripped his hand back and the flame sputtered, sparking, then roared to life to fill the terracotta rutabaga with a glowing light.

Nothing happened. Harry counted to five. Still nothing. "Maybe I lit the wrong one," he said.

"Shouldn't bad things happen when you make a mistake?"

He looked to the pumpkin and the potato. "Or maybe I didn't do enough." He went over to the potato, touched his flame directly to the wick inside it and held it. More sparks, then the flame sputtered and finally caught.

Suddenly, dust billowed from the wall, and he stepped backward, coughing. His boot slipped on the edge of the pool and he nearly tumbled into the water, catching himself at the last moment. He stood teetering on the dry ground. Too close, Harry. He blinked through his tears as stone ground on stone and an opening appeared beneath the glowing rutabaga. Harry coughed again and waved a hand through the dust cloud as he moved forward and knelt for a better look. "I found your soul cake," he called out.

"Bring it here," Lauren called.

"Not sure that's a good idea. It's holding a lever down."

Harry described how the terracotta biscuit sat on one end of a lever inside the newly opened recessed area. Like a playground teeter-totter with a child on only one side, the soul cake kept the long plank unbalanced, with the other end high up in the air. "There's a string connected to the underside of the elevated end," Harry told her. "Take the soul cake off and the lever moves."

"Which causes what?"

"Nothing good is my guess." The Latin writing called for his attention again, and he looked up. *Use* the light of Stingy Jack. Not merely light. *Use* the light. What did Stingy Jack use his light to do?

"Get ready to run." Harry got to his feet, gripped the top of the rutabaga and lifted it.

A new section of stone retracted. It revealed another opening, one cut from the wall to his right. "There's another opening," Harry called out. "And there's something inside."

A cross glimmered inside the new opening. Harry went and picked it up and held it so Lauren could see. "It's white marble," he said. "With writing on it."

More Latin, which he translated as he read. "*Return to the resting place of His Holiness.*"

"That means Pope Sylvester."

She didn't even give him time to think. "I was about to say that."

"Come on."

He stood and looked back to find Lauren had already turned around and begun to walk. "Where are you going?" he called.

She stopped and turned back, looking at him as though he had two heads. "To Rome, of course."

"Rome?"

"To Pope Sylvester."

"You know where Sylvester is buried?"

"You don't?" He ignored that one. "Most Popes are buried in or near Vatican City," Lauren said. "Sylvester should be as well."

"Fine." He set the glowing vegetable down and headed for the stepping stones. "Let's go."

He paused in front of the first step to stick the marble cross in his waistband for security. In doing so, his flashlight beam bounced wildly across the gloomy interior of the cavern, chasing away shadows cast by the glowing terracotta lanterns to his rear. One shadow, however, stayed where it was, calling for his attention. He stepped forward and realized the shadow was more than a shadow. A second message was there on the wall. The northernmost wall.

His boot landed on the first stone as the Latin words went into his brain and turned to English. *Only by following the path farthest from Donn may you cross.*

"Farthest?" His boot landed. The implication hit him. *The message had changed.* "Lauren, do you se—"

Green liquid poured from a drainage hole in the wall beside him. Muck the consistency of sewage spurted out and splashed onto his pants. He leapt without thinking, jumping away from the incoming substance onto a stone in the center row as a scraping noise assaulted his ears. Sparks flashed to life along the roofline, giant sparks that set part of the ceiling ablaze as they fell to the water below. One spark landed on the green ooze. And an inferno erupted.

The inferno spread with terrifying speed. Harry jumped to the next stone as the deadly green ooze continued to pour from every other drainage hole and burst into flame, the heat intense enough to make him lift a hand to ward it off. He leapt ahead again as the water itself burned all around him. A shrieking voice fought through the thick smoke quickly filling this dark chamber. Lauren's voice.

"Get out of there," she cried. "It's Greek fire!"

Greek fire. The deadliest weapon of naval warfare in the ancient world. A liquid stream of death that burned entire fleets in minutes. "I can't get through," he shouted back. "It's everywhere."

Her light was a dim halo in the smoke. "Use the center row."

The step ahead of him burned out of control. Same with the steps on either side. Two steps would get him to safety, but it may as well have been a mile. "I'm stuck," he shouted. "All the steps are on fire."

"The last one isn't," she yelled back. "Over here."

Harry spun around, nearly fell into the burning water, then stood still. Lauren shouted again as one thought ran through his mind over and over. *I'm trapped.*

"Harry!" Lauren shouted his name. "Answer me! I can't see you."

"Middle step in the center," he yelled back.

"I'm coming to you," she shouted.

He didn't have time to consider the insanity of her words before she shouted again. "Jump to the next stone ahead of you."

He could hardly see through the haze. "It's burning," he told her.

"I'll throw my coat over it," she yelled back. "It will cover the fire for an instant. Jump on three."

Harry didn't argue. Lauren shouted the numbers. He crouched, staring into the black wall of smoke, and on *three* he leapt.

His feet hit stone that wasn't burning. He skidded a bit, her coat catching fire as he landed, but Harry kept moving, throwing himself forward through the smoke and onto the last step in the row. Then, he jumped as far as he could through the smoke and heat with no idea what waited.

He crashed into Lauren and sent her tumbling to the ground, then tripped over her legs and landed on her with a grunt and a curse.

"Come on," she cried as she shoved him off and jumped up. "Let's go."

The smoke thinned as they raced up the stairs and out the side of the mountain into the dim light. Lauren caught her foot on the last step, spilling to the ground in front of him. Harry leapt to avoid trampling her again, but his foot caught her shoulder and he slammed to earth, skidding across the dry grass before coming to a stop in a heap.

"I told you they would be here."

A man's voice sounded above him. Harry flipped around to look skyward. Three men looked back down at him. Harry swallowed. *Damn.*

"Well done, Demeter."

Malvolio Buffon stepped in front of the giant called Demeter, a man Harry had last seen submerged in a Florentine river. "Tell me, Harry Fox. What is in the mountain?"

Chapter 11

County Tipperary, Ireland

Harry scrambled to his feet. He blinked, and a pistol appeared in Demeter's hand. An unseen presence made him look to find Lauren had come to stand by his side. Not behind him. Beside him.

"What is inside the mountain?" Malvolio indicated the passage entrance out of which a steady stream of dark smoke poured. "This entrance did not exist before. You opened it, and then you set the mountain on fire. Why?"

Harry looked at the gun. He looked around, finding exactly zero people in sight who could help them. He glared at Malvolio. "You know why."

"Information you found in the library brought you here," Malvolio said.

"I thought that was you in Dublin." Harry shook his head. "How'd you find us?"

"Answer my question."

"Greek fire."

Malvolio blinked. "You have the recipe?"

The man knew his history. "No," Harry said. "I found actual Greek fire, and it nearly killed us."

Malvolio said nothing. He only had eyes for Harry's jacket. Harry glanced down and spotted white stone. *The cross.*

"Give that to me." Malvolio put his hand out.

Demeter waggled the pistol. The third man with them, thankfully not a giant, just scowled. Harry scowled back as he pulled the marble cross from his waist and handed it to Malvolio.

Malvolio held the cross in front of him, angling it toward the sky and bringing the Latin message into view. "What does it say?" Malvolio directed his question to Harry.

Harry shrugged. "No idea."

Malvolio repeated the question to Lauren. She offered a much more colorful response, though she did say she couldn't read Latin either. "Then you are of no use," Malvolio said before turning to Demeter. "Shoot them. Shoot them both."

"Here?" Demeter asked.

Harry jumped in. "What about the dagger?" he asked, his voice even. "You haven't asked about it."

"What dagger?"

Harry nodded his head toward the standing stone. "The dagger I buried on top of that rock."

Malvolio barked at the third man to get his gun out while Demeter retrieved the dagger. The big man went to the top of the stone, pulled the dagger loose—and everyone jumped as the hidden door closed. Demeter came back and handed the dagger to Malvolio.

"Tell me about this dagger," Malvolio said as he held it.

"It's the key to opening the mountainside."

"This was left by Constantine?"

"That's my guess."

"How is it tied to the cross?"

Harry shrugged. "Give me a chance to research that and I'll have an answer."

"Who else knows you are here?" Malvolio asked.

Harry knew when to lie. "All my friends in New York. They know about the cave entrance, too."

Malvolio grunted. "Be quiet."

Malvolio and his crew would hopefully have to take Harry and Lauren elsewhere to dispose of them. Which, Harry fervently hoped, was his chance.

Their rapid Italian exchange filled the air. Harry kept a neutral expression on his face despite understanding every word. Malvolio's plan was to take Harry and Lauren somewhere quiet, ask them questions, and then *get rid of the problem.* Which meant he had a matter of minutes to figure a way out of this jam. No telling how close this quiet place might be, but once they were stuffed into vehicles and taken away, it would get a lot tougher to survive. One problem: Demeter and the other goon were armed. Harry didn't have so much as a knife.

"Move." Demeter shoved Harry in the back, indicating a dirt path. "Down the mountain."

The group set off walking. Lauren and the third captor led the way, Harry behind them, with Demeter on his tail. Malvolio kept pace with Demeter, though when Harry glanced back, he found their leader had his eyes on a phone and not the path. An idea took shape.

They followed the path, moving through tall grass and down occasional rocky slopes for almost twenty minutes until they reached a steeper part of the trail near ground level. They paused at the top of the incline by a standing boulder Harry recalled, one that stood nearly as tall as him and was equally as wide. The contours of the land made this spot virtually invisible from the ground below, at least until you moved down the steep slope. Then it was a straight shot to the ground.

Harry stumbled as they approached the stone. "Whoops!" His arms flailed, he plunged ahead, and with his face leading the way ran smack into the massive stone. A sickly *thunk* sounded before he collapsed on the ground.

Demeter came to Harry's side. "Get up," the big man said.

Harry groaned, cracked an eye. Lauren and her captor stood beside the stone. The third man stuck his gun in his waistband and pulled a small flask from his coat, taking a long swig. Lauren went to Harry's side. "Are you hurt?" she asked.

A groan met her question. She leaned in to check his head. He waited until her face was beside his before he whispered, "Be ready." He winked. Her eyes went wide.

"Get up," Demeter growled half-heartedly. The big man had his eyes on his companion's flask.

"Help me up." Harry shook his head at Lauren when she went to do it. She got the message and backed off. "I need a hand," he said more loudly as he reached toward Demeter. "My head hurts."

The big man swore in Italian before extending one giant paw toward Harry's outstretched hand. Harry bunched his legs up, coiling the muscles as Demeter leaned over. Wait...*now.*

Harry's boot shot out and connected with the inside of Demeter's knee. The man howled, crumpling forward as Harry grabbed his outstretched hand and hurled the big man face-first into the giant boulder. Demeter's head cracked off the rock and he slumped to the ground, out cold. Harry grabbed the pistol from the big man's unresisting hand and turned to fire. A bullet pinged off the rock behind him, needle shards of stone scattering to shoot hot pain across his cheek. Harry shoved Lauren one way, rolled the other, and came up firing as another shot smacked the dirt beside him.

A cry of pain filled the air. Harry's shot had hit the third man's shoulder, sending the man's gun flying. Harry jumped to his feet as Malvolio lunged and plucked the flying pistol from mid-air. A cry of triumph was followed by more shots flying Harry's way. Harry leapt behind the rock to find Lauren already there.

"We can make it to the car," Lauren said as the shooting stopped.

"Not without the cross." Harry poked his head up and was rewarded with a bullet nearly clipping his ear. He returned fire and sent Malvolio leaping to take cover over the lip of the ridge. "There's two of us and one of them. We can get the cross."

"What if he shoots us?"

"I'll get him first."

"No." Lauren pointed to their car. An unobstructed stretch of grass was all that stood between them and escape. "We both run, but not in a straight line, and you keep him busy with suppressing fire. He has two friends who could be ready to fight again at any second. This is our best chance."

"I'm not leaving that cross."

"It's no good to you if you're dead. We'll figure out what it means later."

"How will we keep following the trail?"

"First, survive. Then worry about the rest."

Harry stood and fired a shot, eliciting one in return. "I'm not leaving without the cross. They win if we leave."

"Then sacrifice yourself alone." Lauren turned her back to him. "At least distract him while I run to the car."

"You can't."

"I can, and I will." She spun around so fast he jumped. "Come with me and live to fight another day. Or stay here and die."

Another gunshot split the air and rock shards flew close behind his head. Harry didn't blink. He was a relic hunter, but he also knew common sense when he heard it. Lauren was right. He'd never be the best—and that's what he needed to be—if he died here in Ireland. Harry's mouth turned to a hard line. "Fine. Go. I'll keep them busy."

She ran. He stood, reached over the rock, and fired blindly. Nothing came in return, so he backpedaled, doing his best to keep the gun steady on the ridgeline as he ran sideways. A head popped up into view. Harry fired; the head disappeared. He turned and ran toward the car still several hundred yards distant. Shots sounded behind him as he ran in a random pattern, no longer bothering to fire back even as the shots kept coming his way. He made it and ran at the car as Lauren jumped behind the wheel, ready to roll when he ripped the passenger door open and dove in. Tires spun, rocks flew, and he lunged sideways in his seat to close the car door as she took the turn at speed before roaring down the road, trees racing past on either side.

He waited until they approached a bridge. "Slow down," he said. Lauren did, and when they were halfway across, he tossed his pistol out the window into the creek below and was rewarded with a *splash*. Lauren hit the gas again and they raced off, the evidence buried behind them, along with any chance of recovering the marble cross. The road curved around a bend. Trees gave way to fields, and a highway on-ramp appeared. Lauren raced into the ramp, throwing Harry back in his seat. He clutched the grab handle and gave her a look.

"Time is our friend right now," she said. "Let's use the advantage."

"And get to Rome?"

"Get there ahead of them."

"Then what? We go to Sylvester's tomb and hope?" Lauren's only response was to tell Harry Sylvester was buried in some Roman catacombs. "We need the cross." Harry grumbled to himself and rubbed his temple. They were alive, but they had no path ahead. The white marble cross had revealed merely a location, not what to do next.

Lauren veered into the passing lane and accelerated around a vehicle. "You've uncovered and interpreted the clues so far. Risked your neck to find the next steps," she reminded him.

"I had help." He winked at her.

"You did," she said with a grin. "As much as I would like to take the credit, there's only one relic hunter in this vehicle."

A warmth spread across his chest. "I appreciate having you around," he said.

She let his words linger for quite some time. "I know," she finally said.

Harry waited until she looked at him. He raised an eyebrow. "Why did you never come to Brooklyn to visit?"

More silence. Enough that he was nearly tempted to fill it. "My life is different now," she finally said. Lauren reached up and touched her hair, only for an instant, then put both hands on the steering wheel. "Everything changed after I learned the truth back in that cave."

A cave that had nearly claimed both their lives, and when they ran out of it Lauren had realized her destiny had been written long ago. She was the heir to an ancient Irish throne, and a group of supporters were still trying to put her back on it, even after so many centuries had passed. "You're still Lauren," he said.

A soft grin crossed her face. "If only it were that simple."

"Why isn't it?" he asked, genuinely curious. "Who cares if your ancestors ruled Ireland? That doesn't mean you have to do anything but what you want to do."

"I admire your"—and she seemed to struggle for the word here—"independence. It's so American."

He kept quiet as he puzzled. Was that a dig or a compliment?

"I don't mean it in a negative way," she said. Question answered. "I'm honestly envious. You do what you believe is right. Not what you think you should do."

"Hopefully it's the same thing."

"Not always." She sighed. "After you helped me learn the truth about my organization, about my heritage, I should have felt freedom."

She was referring to her terrible discovery that her employer was far more than a government agency working to raise funds for the Office of Public Works. The entire group, in fact, existed to protect Lauren. Or rather, to protect the blood that coursed inside her. "What did you feel?" Harry asked.

"The weight of expectations. Two thousand years of strangers protecting my family, laying the groundwork to keep our beliefs alive. Generations of people choosing our cause over their own wants and desires." Lauren shook her head. "It's terrifying, Harry. So many people put me, or at least what I stand for, ahead of their own needs. How can I not stand up for what we believe in?"

"Is it what you believe in, or what you think you should believe in?"

Lines creased her forehead. "It's my duty."

"How British of you." She fired a look of anger his way. Harry threw his hands up. "I'm joking. I don't think it's British of you at all. Brits would do it out of a sense of obligation."

"That's what I said I'm doing."

"Which I don't believe." He lowered his hands. "I think you're doing it because you're a good person, and because you believe changing Ireland for the good of everyone matters. You're doing something far better than duty. What you're doing is noble. In every sense of the word."

She laughed long and hard. "Well played, Harry Fox."

"Does that mean you're not coming to visit me in Brooklyn any time soon?"

She looked at him out of the corner of an eye. "It means maybe you don't need to go back there so quickly."

Every train of thought in his mind derailed. "Right." He failed to keep a grin off his face. "I like that."

"Stop gawking at me like a schoolboy and figure out what we do next."

"Right." It took a second to get himself back on track. "There's only one choice I see. Go to Rome."

"What will we do in Rome?"

He hated playing defense. This was a lesson his father had taught him: Control what you can. Prepare for what you cannot. "We let Malvolio and his goons decipher the message on the cross and figure out that Rome is the answer, and we wait for them to come to us."

"Let them do the hard work."

"And while we wait?" Harry drummed his fingers on the dashboard. "We set a trap."

Chapter 12

Rome

Harry's phone buzzed in his pocket. He grumbled silently, taking care not to spill the espresso clutched in one hand as he pulled the device out. A text from his father. *Call incoming in five. Answer it.*

Who's calling me? he replied, but there was no answer. He kept the device in his hand in case the call came early, sipped from the to-go coffee cup, and leaned against the stone wall behind him, closing his eyes and turning his face toward the chilly morning sun. His personal eye of calm in the center of a tourist hurricane.

He and Lauren had taken a midnight flight from Dublin to Rome, arriving before dawn to catch a few short hours of sleep before rolling out of bed at an ungodly hour and venturing out to prepare. Hordes of tourists had yet to descend on the city, but that changed within an hour so that by the time they went out for coffee the streets were filled with visitors. Harry had no idea who would be calling, and right now, he didn't care. He needed a moment for the aches of his adventure to fade and for his brain to kick into gear.

"Ready to go?"

He turned to find Lauren beside him, holding her own cup of coffee. "Let's do it," he said.

Lauren found a cab and they headed toward the northern part of Rome to inspect the Catacombs of Priscilla. It had been his idea to get a room closer to the city. No need to have their home base near the catacombs, not if they wanted a safe place to hide if things went sideways. Assume the worst, he told her. The worst meant Malvolio and his crew had deciphered the message, taken a flight to Rome, and were already at the catacombs. Unlikely, but it could happen. Lauren did not feel the Italian thugs would be that astute.

"I still think we're ahead of them." She uncapped her coffee cup and blew on the steaming liquid as their taxi maneuvered through narrow Roman streets. "We took the last flight of the evening."

"Maybe they have a private plane."

"Where would they get one of those?"

Harry shrugged. "I'm a regular guy who happens to know a rich guy who could get me one."

"Vincent Morello?"

"Shh." Harry waved a hand to quiet her. "Not so loud." He spoke softly. "We have no idea how they found us so quickly at Slievenamon Mountain. That shouldn't have happened. Could be they have more resources than we know."

Lauren had no rebuttal. The taxi bobbed and weaved through traffic until the cabbie deposited them several blocks from the catacombs. Harry's pocket buzzed as his boots hit the pavement. A restricted number showed on-screen. "Hello?"

"Good morning. Are you enjoying our city?"

It took him a second to place it. Italian accent. Impeccable English. A hint of culture in every word. "Cardinal Maldini?"

"I did not expect to find you in Italy so soon."

"How did you—never mind." Of course Cardinal Maldini knew he had returned. Fred Fox knew, which meant Vincent Morello knew, and Vincent would have kept the Cardinal updated. "What's on your mind, Cardinal?"

"A warning. Do you know how the Werewolf Group were able to follow you to the mountain?"

Harry said he did not.

"I am afraid that was our fault."

Harry nearly dropped the phone. "Your fault?"

The reply was soft. "A man close to me betrayed us. A man I trusted."

"And he sold me out?"

"Yes. He was member of my staff," Maldini said, "and his life was threatened."

"Did Malvolio and his thugs threaten this guy?" Harry asked. Maldini's silence was confirmation enough. "You're a powerful man. Have them arrested."

"I cannot prove it. The staff member was accosted by two strangers several days ago. They showed him a picture of his family, then demanded answers to questions about a trail left by Constantine and Pope Sylvester. They also mentioned you by name."

"Why would you tell this guy about my search?"

"I made a serious mistake in trusting my staff," Maldini said. "I am sorry." The Cardinal pressed on. "These men know of your search. They know your name. They did not, however, know where to find you."

"Lucky for them your guy was able to help." Harry waved a hand in disgust. "It's done. We can't change it."

"No, Mr. Fox. We cannot. But I assure you, the Church will assist you in your efforts."

"Because you also want whatever Sylvester left behind," Harry fired back. The Cardinal kept quiet. Harry rubbed his chin. "How about you start by not telling anyone else I'm in Rome?"

"I will tell no one."

"Keep it that way." Harry paused for a moment. "I'm outside the catacombs. Malvolio and his crew have the marble cross we found inside the mountain."

Whatever had been on his tongue fell away as the sun snuck out from between gray clouds overhead, the first real light of the morning washing across the entrance to the catacombs. Buildings painted red fronted the sidewalk, with a metal gate twice the height of a man set beneath a red archway blocking access. The thin metal bars offered an open view of the interior of the property, allowing Harry to look directly into the main catacomb entrance some distance back from the street, on the far side of an open courtyard. Lots of red, plenty of gray stone, but he only had eyes for what sparkled.

"White marble." Harry's words vanished on the chilly breeze. "The interior of the catacombs is filled with white marble."

"That is correct," Maldini said. "Is it important?"

"The cross I found inside Slievenamon Mountain was white marble. Exactly like the catacombs. That can't be a coincidence."

"Why not?"

"My father taught me not to believe in coincidence. Not in the field." Harry rubbed his chin. Malvolio should be en route here soon. Now, most likely. Even those chumps could figure out where to find Sylvester. In fact, Harry wished them the best of luck. "You put me in a bad spot here, Cardinal."

"I am truly sorry for this."

The clouds reconnected to block out the sun. It did nothing to chill Harry's enthusiasm. "Then help me with a problem."

"What do you require?"

"I need a dark room and a trustworthy monk. There's a monastery in front of these catacombs." The red buildings fronting the catacomb entrance belonged to a specific religious order.

"I am familiar with it."

Harry explained what he wanted, when he wanted it, and why it mattered. Maldini didn't speak until Harry finished. "Consider it done," the Cardinal said. "A man will meet you at the front gate within ten minutes."

Harry clicked off and put the phone in his pocket before waving Lauren closer. "I have a plan." He spoke. She listened. "What do you think?" he asked after finishing.

"Are you sure we don't need backup?"

Harry offered a cocky grin. "You don't think I can do this?"

"I think you can be arrogant bordering on confident." Lauren winked at him after intentionally reversing the saying, leaned in and kissed his cheek. "I like it. I'm in."

He led her to the corner of a nearby building down the street from the entrance. They had a view of the gate, but could also duck out of sight if needed. Lauren watched the gate for any sign of the Cardinal's man as Harry kept behind her, unable to silence the question she'd posed. *Do we need backup?* He didn't think so, but Lauren had been spot-on about his hubris. Harry never lacked confidence in the field, something his father reminded him of at times and a fact he couldn't argue with, not honestly. He dialed his father's number. A reality check never hurt.

The call to his father rang through unanswered. Harry tried again. No dice. The phone slowly returned to a pocket. Fred was on his own relic hunt. He didn't have time for another. Harry shook his head. No, his father trusted him to do the right thing. Find the relic, beat these thugs and stop whatever horrors they planned. Would Fred Fox doubt himself? Of course not. Harry's jaw tightened. *Neither will I.*

"Harry."

Lauren's voice pulled him back to the task at hand. "Do you see him?" he asked as he darted to her side.

"The gate just opened."

A man in a black hooded robe that stretched from neck to sandals stepped out of the gate, looked left, then right. Harry stepped into view and walked toward the man. "One side, friend." Harry spoke in Italian as he slipped past the wide-eyed monk and pulled Lauren in behind him. "Please close the gate. They may be here soon."

The monk, who looked barely old enough to vote, fumbled with the gate lock before snapping it shut. "Is someone else there?"

Harry stepped back to get a better look at the monk. This guy was as big and wide as a refrigerator. "You ever play football?" Harry asked in English.

The young man's face lit up and he responded in the same language. "I am the keeper for our monastery team. We are very good."

"The keeper? Oh. Right. Soccer." Football didn't mean football here in Italy. "Listen." He tugged the big man's flowing robe, pulling him toward him, away from the gate. "Did Cardinal Maldini call you?"

"Yes." The single, solemn word made it clear Cardinal Maldini might as well already be a saint. "My name is Nicolo."

"Appreciate it, Nicolo. We need a place to hide. Somewhere with a view of the catacombs' entrance."

Nicolo moved with surprising quickness toward the wall of white marble. He made a quick turn under a covered area and indicated a mural on the wall. Thousands of small chips of colored glass had been adhered to its surface in the shape of a massive cross. "Will this do?"

Nicolo put a hand on the wall and magic happened. The center of the cross fell open at his touch.

"A secret passage?" Lauren asked. "You would never know it existed."

"Not exactly a secret," Nicolo said. "It is a broom closet."

That's when Harry noted the mop handles and yellow buckets hanging on the wall. "It's a big closet," Harry said. "Big enough for us to hide in for a while."

"There is more." Nicolo walked through the false center of the cross and pulled the door shut behind him, making it seem as though he'd never existed. "Can you see me?" Nicolo's voice floated out of the wall. "Hold up your hand. Any number of fingers."

Harry lifted a hand with one finger raised. "One," Nicolo said. "Do it again." This time Harry didn't put his hand up. "Zero," came the reply.

The cross opened. "There is a small hole," Nicolo said, opening the door and stepping out again. "In the door. One piece of glass is missing."

Harry and Lauren inspected the rear of the broom closet door and found the hole in question. "We can stand in there," Harry said, "watch the entrance, and nobody knows we're here."

"Is this good?" Nicolo asked.

"Buddy, it couldn't be better." Harry looked over his shoulder. "No chance we get locked in there?"

Nicolo's head shook. "There is no lock. I will stay close in case you need anything."

"We're looking for two, maybe three men." Harry described Malvolio and the towering Demeter. "They're coming soon."

"The Cardinal said no police."

"That's right," Harry said. "Lauren and I can handle this."

Nicolo said he agreed, though his face told a different story. The helpful monk moved brooms to let them get situated inside the closet and then closed the door. Harry stuck an arm out to stop it from clicking completely shut. "I expect those men will go into the catacombs as soon as they arrive," Harry said. "I'll need you to tell us what to expect down there."

"I would be honored," Nicolo said. "I will be your guide."

"Sounds great," Harry said. "But don't do anything unusual when these guys show up. Act natural if anyone comes around asking questions."

Nicolo grabbed a broom before the door clicked shut. Harry watched the monk sweep as slowly as possible near the closet door, cleaning an already clean floor while keeping one eye on the front entrance. A chime sounded from somewhere inside the monastery, prompting Nicolo to go unlock the front gate and leave it open. He picked his broom up again and swept the ground inside the entrance, cleaning it over and over.

Nicolo's head suddenly jerked up. "Someone is coming through the gate," Lauren said. "I don't have a clear view. Nicolo is in the way." Harry managed to not push her aside. "One person is at the gate. Wait, there are two of them. Two men." Time slowed to a crawl. They waited silently, watching, until Lauren drew in a sharp breath. "They are here."

She moved aside so he could look out. Malvolio and Demeter stood just inside the monastery courtyard. Demeter had a black eye. The white marble cross was nowhere to be seen.

"What are they doing?" Lauren asked.

"Talking. Malvolio just pointed toward the catacomb entrance. Nicolo is watching them while he sweeps. They're not paying attention to him. Hang on." The duo walked closer, stopping when they were directly in front of the hidden closet, not fifteen feet away. "Demeter opened his coat and Malvolio just looked inside it. They didn't take anything out that I could see. I bet the cross is in there, and they're trying to figure out what to do."

The two men stood in place, their heads close as they spoke too softly for Harry to catch anything. Nicolo appeared in Harry's field of vision behind the pair, still sweeping. They didn't take any note of the big monk. "They're moving," Harry said. "Walking to the catacomb entrance."

The white marble façade appeared darker in the gray light as the two men approached, halting before a doorway wide enough for three coffins to be carried through abreast. Malvolio's head moved up and down as he inspected the walls on either side. The rows of decorative columns offered no hints as to why Constantine had left a marble cross. Malvolio turned to Demeter, words Harry couldn't catch were exchanged, and Malvolio led Demeter through the entrance and down the first few steps before they were lost from sight.

Harry counted to thirty before pushing the hidden door open. He signaled for Nicolo to come over. "Did you hear anything they said?" Harry asked.

"Yes," Nicolo said. "The smaller man told the bigger one he could not see any cross. Then he said they must go inside. That is all I heard."

"Good man," Harry said. "What are the catacombs like once you walk down the stairs?"

"It is a single level with two tunnels. Stairs lead down to the tunnel level. From there you can go right or left. Each tunnel is curved and eventually comes back to a place below the outside street. That is where each of them ends."

"What's kept down there?"

"Final resting places for the departed. There are graves set into the wall. They look like shelves. Coffins rest on each shelf. There are three or four from ground to ceiling level, depending on where you are in the tunnel."

"Are the older graves closer to the stairs or to the street?"

"The stairs. Over time we have extended the tunnel toward the street to create more spaces for the burials."

"What are the oldest graves down there?" Harry asked.

"The first brothers were buried not long after Jesus was crucified."

Harry turned to Lauren. "We need to look closer to the stairs. Anything deeper into the tunnels wouldn't have existed in Constantine's time."

Nicolo wrung his hands together. "Are you certain I should not notify the police?"

Harry shook his head. "That would only give those two guys a chance to get away with it."

Nicolo's hands stopped. "What is *it*?"

"I believe there's an ancient statue of Medusa involved," Harry said. "Or maybe not. I'm not sure about that part."

"Why is the statue a problem?"

One of Harry's hands clenched. "The statue is a problem because Malvolio is desperate to find it. I need to know why. I need to stop him." Harry stepped out of the closet. "I'll call you if we need help."

"Phones do not work underground."

Harry grumbled to himself. "In that case, stay near the entrance and don't let anyone go down while we're in there. We'll be back when we're done." Harry frowned. "Nicolo, is there anywhere in the catacombs that's missing a cross? It would be made of white marble, about this big." Harry used his hands to show the size. "I found it and Malvolio took it from me. I think it came from these catacombs."

Nicolo considered. "I am sorry. I do not know of any missing cross."

So be it. Harry went to the top of the stairs and turned an ear toward them, motioning to the others to be quiet. No sounds from below. "Keep everyone out of here until we come back," Harry said. "One more question. Where is Pope Sylvester buried?"

"At a church one kilometer down the road."

Harry went still. "I thought he was buried here."

"He was," Nicolo said. "For hundreds of years. He ordered this monastery to be built specifically for his tomb. Then his remains were moved to the church where they are today. If it is his original tomb you want to see, that is to the right at the bottom of the stairs."

Harry filed that away. "Good to know."

The whine of a distant siren made Harry look at Lauren. She held his gaze. "I will watch your back," she said.

Good enough for him. Harry turned and walked down the steps, Lauren at his heels, the siren's noise fading as the ancient tombs embraced them.

Chapter 13

Rome

Dry air scratched Harry's throat as he reached the bottom step. He moved with caution; even the sound of his breathing seemed to echo off the stone walls. He hesitated as the open staircase that had been hewn from stone came to an end. A low-roofed tunnel branched off to either side, each tunnel curving back *behind* him to either side. Floor-level spotlights had been installed in both branches of the tunnel, casting shadows as they lit the recessed ledges carved into each wall. No sign of the two men.

Harry leaned toward Lauren and whispered, "Where are they?"

Lauren didn't respond. They could have been around the bend in either direction, though how far ahead he couldn't say. The last thing he wanted to do was scuffle with that big thug Demeter in these close confines. He looked toward the closest coffin. A femur might come in handy right now.

"Going right was good advice," Lauren finally said.

"Why?"

"Look at the front of that coffin."

She pointed to the higher coffin to their right, resting around eye level. Harry stepped closer and saw three parallel lines cutting through a layer of dust on the front surface. "Finger marks. One of them touched it."

"Look at the walls further down."

That's when he spotted the faded frescoes of saints and Christian symbols between the stacked coffins. "Do these mean anything to you?" Harry asked.

"I don't see as many paintings going the other way," Lauren said. "Maybe this passage was carved first and reserved for the most important burials."

"Like a pope. Let's look for Sylvester's empty tomb. I'll bet you it's made of white marble."

The ground lighting on either side sent their shadows dancing along the catacomb walls as they walked, the tunnel curving slightly and the coffins growing more plentiful. Less than a minute later Harry spotted an opening in the tunnel wall—a side passage.

"We found it," Lauren whispered.

Harry stopped. "Found what?"

"Look at the painting just inside that opening."

Harry angled his head. "Are those keys?"

"Yes. Crossed silver keys," Lauren said. "The symbol of a pope."

Harry approached the side passage, which ran perpendicular to the main tunnel. As Lauren had said, two crossed keys adorned the curving top of the alcove entrance. The passage stretched perhaps ten feet back from the main thoroughfare. Two soft lights illuminated its interior, one on each side, halfway to the rear wall. The entire passage was covered with white marble.

Harry pointed to the sole decoration in the passage. ""It's the same cross."

A cross of the same marble as the one they had found inside the mountain hung here, on the rear wall. "Same size," Harry said. "Why?" He answered his own question. "It's a marker. It's here"—and here hope bloomed in his chest—"to leave another message."

There was a distinct outline in the marble floor ten feet in front of the back wall. "This is where Sylvester's original sarcophagus sat." But why hadn't it been against the rear wall? Perhaps sconces or statues had once been here. "Keep watch in the passage," Harry told Lauren. "Tell me if you see anyone coming."

"We'll be trapped," she said.

Harry waved her concern away. "I won't take long," he said. He walked toward the rear wall, stopping where Sylvester's tomb had once rested. What had it looked like back then? He imagined a giant marble coffin in the middle of the passage, with candles burning and a stone statue honoring the Pope. No paintings or carvings. Nothing except the white cross.

The stubble on his chin rustled as he rubbed it. He blinked. *Why only two identical crosses?*

Harry reached up, his fingers hovering millimeters away from the cross. The poor light made it hard to see. He leaned closer and pulled on the cross.

The wall moved, inching toward him. He let go, jerking his hand back. It took him a second to understand. This wasn't a wall. It was a *door.*

"Come back here," he hissed.

Lauren quickly appeared at his side. "What is it?" she asked.

"Watch." Harry touched the cross again, but instead of pulling this time, he pushed. With a soft rumble, a rectangle cut into the wall swung back to his touch. Harry pulled hard on the cross and it came loose. He held it securely in one hand and looked at Lauren. She peered into the dark opening.

"The cross was the key," Harry whispered. "You can see the locks on the top and bottom. Pushing it into the wall made those bars retract." A hole on the floor and one on the ceiling marked where it had been deadbolted. Harry pointed at the dusty ground in front of them. "Footprints."

Two pairs of footprints disappeared into the gloomy interior. Harry leaned his head through and turned an ear to the darkness. He touched a finger to his lips and pulled Lauren close. "Hear that?" he asked. She nodded. The echo of what sounded like footsteps came from inside. Harry used his hands to talk. *Follow me. Don't make any noise.* Lauren understood.

He didn't walk in; instead, he waited on the threshold, listening. Faint noises sounded at intervals. A thud that could be a footstep. A quiet murmur that might be a voice. Or was he imagining things? He began to walk, moving silently forward. Lauren followed noiselessly behind. The only light came from behind them, a dim yellowish glow that threw their shadows in front as they walked. An unmarked, curved ceiling overhead was as barren as the walls on either side. They were somewhere beneath the monastery now. Sylvester had built this place specifically to house his tomb. Overseeing the construction allowed him to choose the ideal place to hide whatever else waited at the end of this tunnel. Sylvester and Constantine had wanted the Irish to find this place. They'd made it difficult, but not impossible. Only hard enough to make sure the Irish didn't give up. Which made Harry's heart beat a little faster.

His flashlight showed a sharp turn ahead. He soon glimpsed flickering light, the sort cast by torches in ancient chambers. A light Harry knew well. He stopped just before the turn. The sounds were clear now. A man's voice, too low to make out the words, and still distant. Harry motioned for Lauren to stop.

She pushed him aside and leaned her head around the corner. A breath passed, then she pulled back and put her lips next to his ear. "It's a massive chamber," she said.

Massive chamber? Harry glared at her, leaned around the corner, and what he found took his breath away.

They were at the mouth of a square chamber with ceilings twenty feet high, every surface covered in white marble that reflected the burning torches hanging from sconces along each wall. A tall stone statue waited in the room's center. A man stood in front of the statue with his back to them. A man Harry knew.

"It's Malvolio," Harry whispered.

Lauren's breath warmed his cheek as she replied. "Where is Demeter?"

Harry shrugged. "Not sure. They don't realize we're here."

"We should call the police."

Harry shook his head firmly. "No. We take care of this."

"How?"

Harry hefted the cross in his hand. "I'll distract Malvolio." He handed the cross to her. "You hit him with this."

Lauren was oddly unconcerned with the suggestion. She took the cross. "What about Demeter?"

"I'll worry about him."

Her eyebrows shot up. "He's probably armed."

"I beat him in Florence. I'll handle him here." How, he had no clue, but he kept that to himself.

A soaring central arch supported the high ceiling, which was bisected by a dark line. Two smaller arches with the same dark lines were on either side of the central arch. It looked as though someone had cut through the surfaces with a giant knife. Smoke curled from each torch toward the white stone above.

What stood in the room's center demanded his attention: a statue both hideous and beautiful that dominated the space. Carved of a darker marble than the walls and floor, it showed the soft lines of a flowing robe on a woman's body, while the smooth marble arms and shoulders spoke of her feminine strength. Her face was one of uncommon beauty.

She was a magnificent demon. Snakes writhed atop her head while her eyes pierced the soul. This terrifying monster could turn men to stone with only a look. Harry had never seen a more wondrous creature in his life. *This is the right place.*

Malvolio stood in front of the statue with his back to them, his head raised, peering into Medusa's face. When Harry leaned his head further around the corner, he found Demeter inspecting the odd dark line where it descended from the ceiling and met the floor. Demeter was crouched low, running his hand along the line.

Harry leaned back out of sight and pulled Lauren close. "Demeter's on the right. Here's my plan."

Her mouth tightened, but Lauren didn't protest. She listened until he'd laid it all out. "We should call the police," she said again.

"No. We know Malvolio had at least one man inside the Vatican. Wouldn't he have connections inside the police as well?"

Lauren grumbled and lifted the marble cross. "Fine," she said.

He tried to turn and felt her hand gripping his arm. "What?" he whispered.

"Be careful." She hesitated for an instant, as though her words had stuck in her throat. "I can't do this without you."

The first time he could ever recall her admitting she needed him. "Don't worry." One corner of his mouth turned up. "They'll never know what hit them."

Harry cautiously stuck his head back around the corner to look at the two men. Neither had moved. He motioned to Lauren and she soundlessly hugged the far wall as she entered the chamber. One step, then another, painfully exposed should either man happen to look over. Lauren made her way around the far wall and stopped just outside of Malvolio's peripheral vision. Harry's chest thudded loud enough that he couldn't believe they hadn't heard him. Malvolio had his head down as he studied something in his hands, while Demeter continued to run his finger along the wall, on what Harry could finally tell was an opening in the stone. Lauren stood perfectly still, her eyes on Harry.

Now.

Harry stepped into the chamber. Two steps in and Harry picked up his pace, moving as fast as he could. He made it to within an arm's length of Demeter without being spotted. Harry stopped, opened his mouth and spoke loudly. "Know who that is?"

Malvolio spun around. Demeter twisted, fumbling inside his coat as Harry jumped forward, fists clenched together, and brought them down on the big man's wrist as it came out of his coat. Demeter's gun dropped and clattered away, the big man grunting as Harry pulled back and fired a knee up that glanced off Demeter's chin. Movement flitted at the corner of his vision as Lauren came at Malvolio's back, the white of the marble cross flashing when she lifted it high and brought the heavy cross down on Malvolio's head. Harry didn't watch the man fall. He was too busy throwing a punch at Demeter.

Harry's knuckles cracked off Demeter's jaw. Years in Brooklyn boxing gyms had taught him to hit first and hit hard. Harry followed with three rapid-fire blows to Demeter's kidneys, *left-right-left*. Each landed square; the man's torso was rock hard. Harry pulled his fist down, braced his legs and shot up to fire another direct hit to Demeter's chin that sent a *crack* bouncing off the walls.

Demeter hardly moved. Pain burned in Harry's fist as he leapt back out of range. All Demeter did was growl. "Is that it?" the big man taunted.

Harry gulped. *Damn.* Demeter's eyes narrowed as he looked past Harry. Looked to where his boss lay on the floor. Harry took his chance and went in, fists leading the way, throwing everything he had into an attack on the distracted man. A shot right at Demeter's nose, coming too fast to dodge. A knockout sho—

Demeter threw a forearm up and blocked the punch. Harry stumbled. Demeter fired a jab like a howitzer that crashed into Harry's chest, lifting him off his feet and sending him sprawling to the ground.

"Get back!"

Lauren's shout filled the chamber. She stood over Malvolio, the marble cross held over her head, ready to smash it down again. "Stand back." She waggled the cross to make her point.

Demeter hesitated. He didn't go for his gun, instead looking back and forth from Lauren to Harry.

Harry's chest went tight when a cry sounded behind him. He turned as Lauren fell, her legs swept from beneath her by Malvolio's kick. She went down hard; the marble cross fell from her hand, and before Harry could react Malvolio had a pistol in his hand.

Harry looked back to Demeter. Just in time to see the giant's fist coming straight at his nose.

Chapter 14

Rome

"You are lucky."

Harry shook his head as those words sounded somewhere above his head, echoing in the chamber, pushing through the fuzz wrapping his thoughts. He was flat on his back, courtesy of the haymaker Demeter had delivered to his face.

"I'm not done with you." Harry spat the words out, pulling himself upright in slow motion. His muscles shouted, his entire face ached, and Demeter now had his gun back.

Malvolio wasn't amused. "You two will witness the beginning of it all."

"All of what?" Harry felt like a train had hit him. "The police are coming right now."

Demeter made a noise of fear. Malvolio did not. "You did not call the police," Malvolio said.

Malvolio glared at Harry, who shrugged. "Take your chances," Harry said. "It's not me they're going to throw in jail." *Buy time.* It was their only shot. Harry waved a hand to indicate the statue. "You expected to find a Greek statue down here?"

"It is beyond everything I hoped for."

Apparently Malvolio knew as much as Harry. "Good luck getting it out of here." Harry checked his watch, the movement making his head spin. "You should run now. Time's almost up."

The gunshot made everyone jump. Lauren shot to her feet as marble exploded by Harry's boot and shards filled the air. "Enough!" Malvolio shouted. "You have one chance. This room"—and here Malvolio waved at the statue and the opening across the walls and ceiling. "It is a mystery. The answer to why it exists is here." Malvolio pointed to a spot by Medusa's feet. "The inscription. I assume you now read Latin. What does it say?"

What was he talking about? Harry stepped forward and found a rectangle of green stone had been laid into the floor in front of Medusa. A Latin inscription ran across the stone at her feet. *Malvolio can't read Latin.* Harry walked over and knelt in front of the statue, taking his time.

"This references the Medusa story," Harry said. "And the man who killed her. It says '*Look at the demon as Perseus did.*'"

Malvolio took a phone halfway out of his pocket, frowned, and jammed it back in. "Tell me how well you know the story," he demanded.

No cell service down here. And Malvolio didn't know the myth of Perseus. "Medusa was a Gorgon," Harry said without hesitation. "One of three sisters whose gaze could turn men to stone. The only mortal sister, the only one who could be killed. A king who wanted to marry Perseus's mother sent Perseus to kill Medusa, which should have been a suicide mission. Lucky for Perseus the gods decided to help him."

"The gods could have just killed her for him," Malvolio said.

"The gods need entertainment. They leveled the playing field and helped Perseus." Harry studied the twisting stone snakes atop Medusa's head. Each snake had an open mouth that was a dark hole. Holes, all the same diameter, each one pointing directly at Harry as he stood in front of the statue. *Interesting*. His next words came out softly. "They gave him gifts."

Harry stood carefully and turned. Demeter's pistol came up and the giant made it to Harry's side quickly, standing just out of arm's reach. "Easy," Harry said. "I'm looking for something." It only took a second. *How did I miss it?* "That."

He pointed to a convex circle in the chamber wall. Two feet in diameter, at chest height, a marble circle easy to overlook. Harry ignored Demeter as he walked directly to the circle. The round outline proved deep. Harry poked a finger into the opening and found no end. He took his phone out and used the flashlight to peer into the crevice. The groove in the wall seemed to have no bottom.

He checked the entire circle. Other than a connection at the very top and bottom, the circular outline was a bottomless chasm. Harry stepped back. His hand rustled the stubble on his chin. This isn't decorative. It has a purpose. Why only connect it at the top and bottom? He looked back at the Medusa statue directly behind him. "It's meant to be a shield."

Malvolio shouted at Harry to speak up. Harry ignored him and touched the wall. He pushed. His eyes widened.

Without a word he put both hands on the right edge of the circle, just inside the line, and pushed. Stone that had lain stationary for millennia protested as it spun. The circle rotated on a central axis, rotating until the opposite side of the stone now faced outward. Where moments before the stone circle had bulged outward, it now curved inward.

Harry stood back. "It's a shield. The same as in the myth. This opposite side is polished so it's brighter." Bright enough to make his eyes narrow. "This is how Perseus looked at Medusa. He used—"

A grinding noise rumbled behind him. Demeter shouted as Harry turned to find the big man stumbling away from the statue. Harry tensed as the front of Medusa's stone dress slid back to reveal a chamber inside the statue.

"It does exist." Malvolio pushed Lauren aside as he stepped toward the figure. "It is all true."

Green and white light erupted from inside Medusa. A miniature version of the elegant, demonic horror that was the Gorgon stood in the hidden chamber. Fearsome golden snakes writhed between stunning emeralds. The serpents' flicking and probing tongues were of the same green as the stones they encircled, while each snake's two emerald eyes sparked with a demonic emptiness. A chill ran up Harry's spine.

"There's a message," Harry said. Dark green letters ran across the polished interior. Latin letters, dark green. The same green as the rectangle on the floor in front of Medusa. "*Honor the Eucharist to retrieve heathen icon.*"

Lauren found her voice. "The statue. Constantine is returning the statue."

"To the Irish king," Harry said. "Which the Irish had gifted to Constantine as a commitment to keep the peace."

Malvolio didn't appear to listen. "It is mine," he said. "It will change everything."

A diabolical energy emanated from Malvolio's expression, one that mirrored Medusa's ability to make Harry's chest tighten and his nerves come alive. "It's a demon statue the pagan Irish gave to an emperor," Harry said. "Their effort to keep from being slaughtered. It didn't work. You want to pin your future on this?"

Malvolio waved a hand to dismiss Harry. "Our time has come." He barked at Demeter. "Get it."

The big man hesitated, then turned to Harry. "What does that mean?" He used his pistol to indicate the message on the shield. "What honor?"

Harry barely heard the question. The message on the shield. Of the same green as the floor fronting Medusa. Why? His father had taught him coincidence didn't exist for a relic hunter in the field. *Honor the Eucharist.* The Christian ceremony commemorating the Last Supper, a ritual that played out in thousands of churches across the globe, bread and wine first consecrated by a priest before being consumed by the faithful. Honor the Eucharist. Harry closed his eyes. He saw only snakes.

His eyes snapped open. "It's an insult." Harry turned to Lauren as he spoke. "An insult from the Pope to the pagan Irish."

Sparks erupted from the burning torch nearest Harry, ancient accelerant catching to give the fire urgency and cast a brighter glow where he stood. Shadows covering the shield vanished and revealed a new feature. Another inscription had been etched into the white marble, below the dark green letters and so small he'd missed them. Harry read the Latin phrase silently. *Thrice the Lord will punish the pagan as he did Leviathan. The icon calls his terrible swift sword.*

Leviathan, the swiftly moving serpent from the Book of Isaiah. The Bible foretold God chopping the snake to pieces. Now that same vengeance was being directed at *the pagans.* The Irish pagans.

"The demon statue is ours." Malvolio aimed his pistol at Harry's chest to make the threat clear.

Harry's mind churned. *Thrice?* What had to be punished three times? Did it mean God would somehow strike down Medusa, or the Irish pagan king whose gift of the statue signified only peace?

"What do you want the demon statue for?" Harry asked. Best way to buy time was to get them talking.

Malvolio glared at him. "You have no concept of what this will mean. To me. To my people." He waved the pistol in a circle. "Our movement will topple everything you hold dear."

Thrice. Something about three mattered. "Hate to break it to you," Harry said. "If you're talking about this monastery, I'm not a member."

"Such a small thought from a small man," Malvolio said. "The curse of your kind."

"My kind?" Harry didn't have to put any false venom in his words.

"The inferior race," Malvolio said. "Your weakness is written all over you."

"That's funny, coming from you." Time to put Malvolio on the back foot. "You think this demon statue will persuade people to abandon the Church? They'll laugh at you. Another chump with a crazy idea who blames everyone but himself for his troubles. Besides"—and here Harry winked—"we look pretty much the same."

A gunshot boomed and the bullet zipped past Harry's face, far too close for comfort. Harry ducked, arms over his head. "Look who is joking now," Malvolio said. "I know the Church sent you. They are afraid. How do you think I found you on the mountain?"

"Threatening an innocent person." Harry brushed dust off his arm. "You're a B-movie gangster from an eighties flick. The one who dies in the end."

Malvolio growled something in Italian Harry didn't catch. "Watch what is to come," Malvolio said in English. He turned to Demeter and barked for his henchman to grab the demon statue.

The big man shrugged, greed flashing on his face as he walked toward the waiting icon, stopping directly in front of the large Medusa statue and reaching inside for the glimmering demon, about the size of a shoe. Both of his feet were on the green rectangle. Harry glanced at Lauren. Her face was tight. Harry splayed the fingers on his hand. *Wait.*

Demeter leaned forward and his fingers wrapped around the bejeweled golden statue. The world paused, Harry blinked, and Demeter lifted the statue from inside the marble Gorgon with an audible grunt. "It's heavy," he said.

The Gorgon's serpentine hair coiled and struck. Demeter gripped the demon statue for no more than a second before Medusa's stone hair erupted with a death knell. Arrows shot from the open mouths of the stone snakes on her head, metal projectiles flying on a path for Demeter as he stood directly in front of the statue.

Lauren's cry cut off a beat after it sounded. She lifted a hand to her mouth, her eyes open, not moving from her position by Malvolio, who stood rooted to the ground, the pistol frozen in his hand, his entire body rigid. He did not move as Demeter's massive frame collapsed in a heap. The brilliant demon statue landed on the marble by his corpse.

Harry ran to Demeter's lifeless body, breathing hard and waving his hands, a man shocked at the sight of such horrors, a man reacting to tragedy. Not a man looking to scoop up a gun dropped by a body.

A gun buried, alas, beneath the dead man's considerable bulk. Harry made a show of touching Demeter's neck to check for a pulse, all the while looking frantically for the pistol. *It must be here.* He shoved the heavy corpse and the gun's metal glinted in the firelight, poking out from beneath Demeter's shoulder. Harry leaned into the corpse, shoving until the gun was exposed. His fingers touched the cold metal.

A gunshot split the air and Demeter's body jerked. "Get back!"

Harry lifted his hands. Malvolio aimed his gun at Harry and repeated the command. Harry stood, keeping his hands up, but he didn't move back from the body. "Medusa shot your friend," Harry said.

Malvolio's face burned red. "No. You killed him."

"Me?" Harry asked. "I had no idea those snakes were loaded."

"Constantine and Sylvester put that icon here for the pagan Irish to find," Malvolio said. "It was a trap to kill the Irish, and you knew about it." Malvolio grabbed Lauren by the shoulder and threw her toward Harry. She stumbled, catching herself before she collided with the stone statue. "What did you not tell me?"

"I told you everything," Harry said. "Ask her if I did." Harry indicated Lauren. "She reads Latin too."

Malvolio waved Harry into silence. "All that matters is the icon." His teeth flashed as he pointed at the fallen treasure. "Pick it up."

A groaning sounded somewhere above them. Malvolio didn't blink, but Harry did. Clouds of dust fell from the ceiling, coming from one of the dark, open arches that ran from one side of the room to the other. *Three arches.* Harry drew in a sharp breath and whispered to himself. "Three terrible swords."

Malvolio stuck his hand out. "Get the icon. Throw it to me."

More dust fell. "You want it?" Harry asked. He picked up the icon from near his feet. "Catch."

Harry threw the icon high and long as the groaning sounds turned to a roar. A giant double-headed axe erupted from the central archway and arced across the chamber at speed.

Malvolio tripped as he lunged for the flying statue. As he fell, the blade's finely honed edge whispered past him, missing him by a hair as it flew toward the far side of the room, continuing up and out of sight.

The gun. Harry jumped toward Demeter's corpse as Malvolio struggled to regain his feet. Harry bent over to frisk the corpse once more, and he saw light glinting off the pistol, which lay inside the floor channel, out of reach.

"Harry!"

Lauren's hands were outstretched, reaching for him, as Malvolio grasped her ankle, yanking her back. She gave Malvolio a hard kick and he let her loose with a yelp. She stood, took one step and went still. "Watch out!" she cried.

Harry looked over his shoulder and found the axe on its return journey across the chamber. He threw himself back as Lauren did the same, the two of them diving in opposite directions to avoid being sliced in half as the blade swept past. Lauren flattened herself on the floor of the chamber, and Harry stood to one side of her. Malvolio leapt aside, taking several steps back to stand above a prostrate Lauren. His pistol was aimed at Harry. "Know that your life was not a waste," he said. "You led me to the icon. You played a role in the revolution to follow."

Malvolio closed one eye and leveled his pistol. Dust sparkled above Harry. He looked down at the gap in the floor, the gap closest to the door. Movement fluttered at the edge of his vision, off to the left. He took a small step back and grinned. Malvolio hesitated. "The fascists lost," Harry said. "So did you."

Malvolio pulled the trigger at the same time as a giant axe swept out of the wall in front of Harry. Metal struck metal, the bullet pinging off this new axe that passed in front of him to block the shot.

Harry sprinted at Malvolio as the Italian ducked and the final axe came out of the wall.

Lauren began rising to her knees, bringing her directly into the blade's path. Harry planted his foot on the marble, switched course, and Malvolio moved back. An instant too late.

Harry slammed into Lauren to knock her out of the way. They flew clear, hit the ground, and Harry turned to find Malvolio on the ground, neatly severed in half, one piece of him lying to either side of the room's center. He would not be getting back up.

Harry grabbed Lauren's arm and pulled her aside before the third axe could swing back, scooped up the demon statue, and raced through the chamber door with Lauren right behind him.

Epilogue

Vatican City

"Please sit on the towels. We hope to avoid leaving blood on these chairs. They are quite old."

Harry accepted the ruby-red bath towel that Cardinal Roberto Maldini handed to him. Lauren did the same, both putting the towels down on chairs that each cost more than Harry's college education. The Cardinal's words echoed in the cavernous room. They were the only three people present. Two guards in civilian dress had left moments ago to stand watch just outside the towering doors. The assault rifles each had strapped over their shoulders would likely keep interruptions to a minimum.

Roberto stood before them, arms behind his back. "Is there anything you require?" he asked, not unkindly.

"An explanation." Harry's voice brooked no dissent. "About everything." He paused. "And thanks for picking us up." Lauren echoed the sentiment.

"I preferred to discuss this in private," Roberto said. "Instead of at the monastery or with the authorities. Their questions may be difficult to answer."

Harry had run into Nicolo immediately after escaping from Emperor Constantine's chamber of terror. He told the young monk to keep anyone from entering the hidden hallway or the chamber, then asked him to call Cardinal Maldini. A Mercedes sedan had appeared outside the monastery faster than should have been possible. Harry and Lauren were whisked to a back gate in the outer perimeter of Vatican City before being led by machine gun–toting Swiss Guards to this expansive ballroom, where Roberto had been waiting. No one had spoken until the Cardinal handed them the luxurious towels and asked them to sit.

"What happened in the chamber?" Roberto asked.

"Did Nicolo tell you?" Harry asked. Roberto shook his head. "Then you'll want to see this." He inclined his head toward Lauren.

Lauren removed the statue from inside her coat and the Cardinal gasped. "You found it."

The statue seemed to radiate light on the table, every emerald glistening and the gold sending soft flares of brilliance off every inch of it. A beautiful demon had arrived inside the heart of Christendom. A demon, strange as it seemed, which was welcome.

"You can't have it." Harry crossed his arms and gave Roberto his best glare. "It's ours."

Roberto didn't even look at Harry. "I wouldn't dream of asking for it. This incredible artifact was created as a sign of peace between two faiths."

"A peace your Pope had no interest in offering," Harry said. "Which you knew."

That got his attention. "I knew no such thing."

"Then how did you know to warn me about the 'terrible swift sword'?"

Roberto stood and put his hands behind his back. "I will answer your question. But first, tell me what happened beneath the monastery."

Harry did. A concise summary, sparing no details on how they had nearly died several times. Roberto let him talk without interruption. Only after Harry finished did Roberto ask about the messages on the statue, on the floor and on the reversed shield.

"The first message on the shield was in green," Harry said. "The same vivid green as the floor. That's how I knew Demeter was in trouble."

"He wasn't kneeling when he reached for the icon," Roberto said. "Had he knelt, the arrows would have flown over his head."

"The messages on the shield were the same green color," Harry said. "And only a Christian would understand them. Odds are an Irish pagan king wouldn't have known about the Eucharist. However, they would have known the story of Medusa and how Perseus used the shield's reflection to kill her. If you don't know the story, the arrows get you. Or the axes, if you get lucky. That's what Constantine and Sylvester wanted to happen."

"Leaving the terrible swift sword of our Lord to exact further vengeance."

Lauren had been seething quietly. No longer. "On a people who wanted nothing more than peace," she fired back. "Sylvester sent them on a deadly journey to retrieve what they believed was a peace offering. They were never meant to survive. It was a trap." Her words grew hot. "Why? To stamp out a rival religion. They wanted to destroy the leaders of paganism."

Harry jumped in. "Which makes recruiting the pagan believers easier."

Roberto stood still. "It is not what I would have done," he finally said before turning to Harry. "As to your question, I did not know of the danger in store."

"Then why did you quote the exact passage I needed when we spoke?"

"The Lord works in mysterious ways."

"I think there's more to it than that," Harry said. "I think this entire journey was meant to send a message to the Irish."

"That message being?"

"That your church would destroy them no matter what." Harry raised a hand and began ticking off his proof, one finger at a time. "First, how to banish a wulver in the Clava Cairns. Fire is the answer, not a silver dagger, because fire would scare the wulver away. Wulvers didn't hurt humans. Using silver to kill a wulver, or werewolf, was an idea that wasn't developed until centuries later. Second, lighting a rutabaga tied to Stingy Jack inside Slieveneman Mountain, which we only found because of the poison plants that grew on it."

Lauren interrupted. "A poison plant that reminds us that witches were seen as evil, when in truth they helped people. The mountain's name should honor those women, not vilify them. And don't forget the Greek fire that nearly killed us."

"Which all leads back to your Pope," Harry said. "A Pope who left a trap meant to kill the pagan leaders and leave the faithful adrift. Sylvester and Constantine worked together to force the Irish to assimilate against their will."

"But they failed." Lauren's words were daggers aimed at Roberto. "This isn't just a story about Halloween, about pumpkins and witches and candy. It's about my people. Your Pope used their icon as bait to lure them to their deaths."

Silence returned. Roberto held their gaze. He did not argue. He watched them as they watched him. He waited.

The phone between them chimed. Roberto lifted the receiver, held it to his ear, then set it back down without a word. "I understand your anger and appreciate your position," he said. "Perhaps you will listen for a moment?"

Lauren waved a hand in disgust, indicating that he was free to speak.

"Thank you," Roberto said. "Much of what you say has merit. However, please consider this. The man who challenged you on this journey is—*was*—evil incarnate. Malvolio Buffon wished to destroy the Church and foster fascism. He was closer to succeeding than we realized."

"He couldn't destroy the Church," Harry said.

"No, though he could permanently damage us and the faithful through many cuts. Men in our service located Malvolio's hidden broadcasting facility this morning." Roberto nodded to Harry. "You recall the repulsive podcast playing in my car when we met?" Harry said he did. "That man's identity was unknown." Roberto took a phone from inside his garments and displayed an image. "This mask was found alongside the broadcasting equipment, along with clear evidence that Malvolio was the man who wore it."

A red skeleton mask appeared on Roberto's phone. "This mask belonged to Malvolio. He was the man spreading so much hate."

"Not any longer," Harry said.

"For which the Church owes you a debt," Roberto said. "His group has been dealt a fatal blow. It will fade away without his guidance."

Knocking sounded on a side door. "Would you do me the courtesy of standing?" Roberto asked. Harry looked at Lauren, who glowered as she rose. He did the same. "A man wishes to speak with you," Roberto said.

The small door opened. Two men in red robes walked through. More cardinals? This couldn't be good. They stood on either side of the door and stayed in place. A pair of Swiss Guards toting assault rifles came next. Harry's nerves came alive. *What's going on?*

One more person walked through the door. A small man, wearing glasses, with a plain robe of bright white. A man whose face was known across the globe.

Roberto lowered his head briefly. "Welcome, Your Holiness."

The Pope made the short journey to stand before them, both guards flanking him, their backs straight and their eyes ahead. "Hello." He spoke in impeccable English. "Welcome to our home."

What did you say to a pope? Harry stuck his hand out, pulled it back, then dipped his head briefly. "Hello, Your Holiness." Lauren did the same when the Pope turned to her.

"We owe you our thanks." The Pope indicated the Medusa icon. "I have prayed for your safety these past few days."

Harry, whose faith could be described as tentative on a good day, nearly fell over. "You did?"

The Pope smiled. "All of our prayers have been answered." Harry couldn't think of a single thing to say, so he kept quiet. "I have a favor to ask," the Pope continued. "Of you both."

They nodded dumbly. "This icon," he said. "Would you allow me to borrow it?"

Harry knew few things with certainty in life. One thing he did know was that having the Pope owe you could be useful. Very useful. "Of course," Harry said. "If Lauren agrees."

They both turned to Lauren. "Certainly," she said. Then lightning struck. "On one condition."

The Pope raised a bushy white eyebrow. "Yes?"

Lauren forged ahead, heedless of the fact that actual lightning might hit her at any moment. "I'm running for a seat in the Irish House of Representatives."

"The Dáil Éireann. I know."

"You do?" Her face screwed up for an instant. "I would be most grateful if you would put in a good word for me with the right people."

The Pope's eyes sparkled with mirth. "A strong young woman." He gave a mock frown. "You are a Catholic?"

"Yes."

The mirth spread to the rest of his face. "In that case, I shall have a word with my friends."

Lauren nodded. "Thank you."

The two guards stepped back as the Pope bade Harry and Lauren farewell before exiting as quietly as he had entered, his retinue in tow. The gentle click of the door closing stirred Roberto from his silence.

"I expect you are both tired," he said. "May we offer you a ride home?"

Fog still clouded Harry's mind. "To Brooklyn?"

"If you wish."

Harry opened his mouth. He closed it. This was the Vatican they were dealing with. Of course they could get Harry back to Brooklyn. Harry nodded. "I'd appreciate that." His heart jumped and he turned to Lauren. "What about you?"

She looked at Roberto. "I'll need a flight to Dublin, please. And would you give us a moment?"

"Your cars will be waiting outside," Roberto said. He turned and left, closing the large door behind him.

Lauren took one of Harry's hands in both of hers. "I'm sorry, Harry."

"For what?"

"You know." She sighed and ran a hand through her hair, her eyes going to the floor for an instant before returning to his. "It seems fate has other plans for us."

"Like you becoming an Irish politician and me continuing to be a guy from Brooklyn?"

"You are far more than that." She squeezed his hand. Her lips opened slightly.

His phone buzzed. "It's my dad."

"Take the call." She dropped his hand, turned, then spun back around before he connected it. "And say he can wait one more day. I'll push the flights until tomorrow." She winked. "We're in Rome. We should spend at least one night in the city."

"We should?"

"You haven't taken me out to dinner yet."

With that, she left. Harry stood dumbfounded as the phone in his hand continued to buzz. Lauren was a handful. And lucky for him, she wasn't ready to leave him just yet.

The phone stopped buzzing, then immediately started again. He connected the call. "Hey, Dad."

Fred spoke without missing a beat. "You know, I always wanted to meet the Pope."

"How in the world do you know that just happened?"

"Cardinal Maldini just called Vincent. He said you gave the Pope a gift."

"It was Lauren's idea. I wanted to keep it."

"Keep what?"

Harry laughed. "I'll tell you when I get home. Which won't be for another day," he said quickly. "Maybe two." Who knew? A guy could hope.

"Don't be too long."

Something in his dad's voice made him take note. "Why not?"

"I have something you'll want to see."

The hair on his neck went up. "You're talking about a relic."

"No relic." A pause. "Not yet, at least. I bought a papyrus scroll from the Roman Empire this week. I'm interested in the fresco on the document, but after I purchased it, I found it contained more than a portrait." Fred paused. "It's a palimpsest."

Harry drew in a sharp breath. A palimpsest. A piece of writing material or a manuscript that had been written on once and then reused for another document, with the original writing often scraped off or otherwise erased. Such artifacts could contain anything. Including lost works by scholars or writers. "The owner didn't know?"

"Let's say he wasn't the most discerning of collectors."

A black-market deal, then. All the better for Fred. "Is it another Archimedes codex?" Harry asked. He was referring to the famous example of a document hiding copies of two lost works by the greatest mathematician of all time.

"Not quite. This hidden text is a story about Saint Nicholas."

It took him a second. "The patron saint of sailors?"

"The very same. It seems Saint Nicholas may have left more behind than the inspiration for a certain jolly man in a red suit."

Jolly man? It took him a second. "You mean *Santa Claus?*"

Fred chuckled. "I should call him Saint Nick. Yes. The man whose supposed gift-giving inspired the folklore behind Santa Claus." Fred's response made Harry's skin tingle. "A story that tells me Saint Nick had an incredible treasure in his sack. Better than any Christmas present you could imagine. And the best part? It's real, it's out there, and I might know how you can find it."

Author's Note

I must admit one fact up front: my very favorite holiday of the year is Halloween. I couldn't *wait* to dive into this story when I came up with the idea for holiday-based Origin Stories, though the more I dug into the history of this ancient holiday, the less it became about the costumes and ghouls and all the fun stuff we're familiar with. The roots of Halloween are deep in our past. They cross civilizations, stretching to a time when the world was a far more frightening and mysterious place. A time when humans knew very little about nature, science or the universe in general. This lack of knowledge was a void people filled with a mix of superstition, guesswork or outright fantasy. A time when the candle of knowledge pushing back the darkness of uncertainty and fear did not burn nearly so bright as it often does today. A time when – I am certain – the boundaries between our world and whatever is on the other side was thin. Perhaps that boundary broke once or twice and a man or woman standing at the edge could glimpse what waited, and if they did, help shape the stories that led to a holiday that has shaped the modern world.

What are the likeliest origins of modern Halloween? It depends on who you ask. One theory, which I'll go so far as to call the prevailing theory, is that most modern Halloween traditions tie back to Celtic harvest festivals, specifically a Gaelic festival called Samhain which marked the end of the harvest season and the beginning of winter, when the days grew short and the nights long. Samhain celebrations began on the evening of October thirty-first (sound familiar?). Samhain itself likely grew out of Celtic Pagan rituals and beliefs, though those are quite a ways back in the historical record and we simply don't have a ton of great evidence as to if it's accurate or not, so I'm beginning my summary with Samhain.

Important to Harry's story are the Irish myths associated with Samhain. In these myths, Samhain was a time when the doors or portals between worlds could open to allow mythical creatures, souls of the dead or supernatural entities to cross between their world and ours. When you consider how frightening the ancient world must have been to our ancestors – imagine facing the dark days of winter with no electricity or running water – it's not hard to see how myths sprang up about dead people coming back for a visit. Slightly comforting, but high on the terror scale as well.

A specific Irish myth Harry ran across in this tale involves a hero named Fionn mac Cumhaill and his exploits with slaying a fire-breathing creature named Aillen – more on that later. For now just know it's a real myth and Fionn made his name saving everyone's backside from being toasted.

Back to Halloween origins and our modern holiday. The theory of Samhain serving as the inspiration for Halloween also indicates the celebration of Samhain was appropriated by the Christian church. When this happened isn't clear, though like most historical transitions, it didn't happen all at once, instead shifting slowly from what Christians would have called Pagan beliefs to more Christian themes over time. At a point after the fall of the Western Roman Empire in the fifth century, stretching until the ninth century, Christian leaders and missionaries began holding a festival at the same time as Samhain.

Evidence of this intentional co-opting includes a letter from Pope Gregory I in the sixth century advising non-Christian places of worship be used for Christian worship, and what easier way to slowly replace Pagan beliefs with Christianity than by replacing an existing holiday with one of your own? In this theory, Samhain became All Hallows' Eve (or Day, which is November first) and the Pagan celebration eventually vanished.

Following that, over time and mainly in Europe, various countries and cultures added their own twists to the celebrations. Samhain never died out entirely, including the giant bonfires lit for the celebration to ward off the coming dark and to light the path for returning souls of loved ones, and this tradition was supplemented by new ones. One example was found in Ireland and Scotland, when celebrants would dress in costume and go house-to-house singing in exchange for food. As to the origins of jack-o-lanterns, the Stingy Jack myth discussed in this story is real and is a strong contender for the tradition beginning in Europe. The practice of carving pumpkins spread to North America in the nineteenth century, helped in no small part by Washington Irving's *The Legend of Sleepy Hollow*, adaptations of which often featured the Headless Horseman with a jack-o-lantern in place of his head.

The only certainty regarding how modern Halloween came to be is that multiple cultures, geographic regions and motivations led to us enjoying trick-or-treating in costumes today. To me, that's the perfect mix for a Harry Fox adventure, and as we do after every story, let's separate fact from fiction.

The impetus for Harry Fox diving into the world of ghouls and goblins is a sword which Constantine the Great offered to a Brittonic tribal leader (*Chapter 1*) as a gesture of peace, a sword he named after the Irish mythical hero Fionn mac Cumhaill. According to legend Fionn slayed a fire-breathing invader each year with that sword. While the myth exists and Fionn did supposedly bring down a massive man who breathed fire once per year, in truth there were never any substantive peace discussions between the Roman Empire and the peoples of Brittania, which existed as a Roman province during Constantine's reign – it was in fact occupied by Rome for nearly four hundred years. First invaded by Julius Caesar around 55 BCE in the Gallic Wars, Rome continually committed troops to fend of invaders they termed barbarians, who in truth were a diverse group of peoples after the fertile land for themselves. The last Roman forces eventually withdrew from what is now Britain around 410 ADE.

The story of how the fascist villains in this tale came to be known as the *Werewulf* Group (*Chapter 2*) is based on a true story. The term *Werwolf* was used as the moniker for an actual Nazi plan developed near the end of WWII, whereby Nazi-aligned resistance forces would operate behind Allied lines as they advanced toward Germany, engaging in clandestine operations to undermine their enemy. Allied forces had similar groups, though the Allied operations expanded operations to a much greater extent than the Nazi version. The Werwolf groups may have carried out several assassinations in the closing months of the war, also possibly destroying a handful of Allied facilities, but their ultimate impact was minimal compared to what had been planned. I thought it was a perfect name for the villains in this story for obvious reasons.

The Werewulfs in this tale recruit disaffected youths (*Chapter 4*) who don't have a place in society and want a group to which they might belong. Such tactics are quite common for subversive and radical groups around the world, used even today by neo-Nazi factions in the United States, Europe and other areas. The attraction of belonging is quite powerful for those who do not necessarily fit neatly into society, face challenges socializing with others of their age, or perhaps who are unable to form any sort of romantic relationship. These groups use that insecurity and loneliness to drive what are otherwise kind people to commit horrific acts. It is as common a method of recruitment today as it was a thousand years ago, and until we as a society are able to help those most in need of finding their place in society, it will continue to wreak havoc across the world.

The Clava Cairns (*Chapter 5*) in which Harry and Lauren must vanquish a Wulver are real, thought the Skull Cairn is not. I created that specific cairn for the purposes of this story. The god Aed, who aids in their quest to uncover the truth, is in fact the Irish mythical god of underworld. However, the wulver legend they reference to follow the trail is only one of many possible origins for werewolves, as the concept of a person who changes into a wolf-like creature is widespread in European folklore. As to silver for a way to kill or combat lycanthropy (which comes from the Ancient Greek term for "wolf-human") that is only one of many ways to handle a werewolf. Other ways to ward them off include exhaustion, exorcism or, my personal favorite, scolding. The story of the Wulver in this tale, at least the version I reference where they fish a lot, is true except for bonfire part. Also factual is the myth about Stingy Jack, but I adjusted the timing of this myth as in truth it wasn't recorded until the nineteenth century, fifteen hundred years after Constantine's time.

The Loughcrew Cairns (*Chapter 9*) are real, as is Slievenamon Mountain, thought it is not referred to as the mountain of the witch. However, the idea that one possible origin of the word witch is in fact a mistranslation of the word poison is real. This comes from a possible improperly translated word in the Christian Bible which states *thou shalt not suffer a witch to live.* Some scholars believe the original intent was to say *poisoner* instead of *witch*, though that is still up for debate. The standing stones at the mountain are not real, I made them up, but the cairn on top of Slievenamon is real. As to if there is a hidden cavern containing an ancient cross which may only be retrieved through knowledge of the Stingy Jack myth, well, I am not certain either way. Please let me know if you should uncover the truth when you are on the mountain.

Harry's knowledge of Irish myth is further tested when he must know that Donn is the god of the underworld (*Chapter 10*). This is true, and Donn does rule the mythical Irish underworld, but the story about taking the south path to visit the underworld is my creation for story purposes and not real. Samhain is about honoring the dead, and some myths did say their spirits could return to the world of the living, but I created up the part about them taking a southern route. In regards to soul cakes, the practice of asking for soul cakes in exchange for prayers for the departed didn't become widespread until the fifteenth century, well after it would have needed to be in practice for Constantine to incorporate it into his dangerous path.

The climax of Harry's scene takes place in the Catacombs of Priscilla (*Chapter 12*). As a factual aside, the Catacombs are real, having originally been a quarry in Ancient Rome. The Catacombs extend for over seven miles and are one of the most extensive in the city. The modern entrance is truly in a Benedictine monastery, the buildings of which are red, though there is no white marble façade or entrance. Pope Sylvester really was originally buried here, but his remains have since been moved to another church in Rome. If there is a hidden entrance leading to a secret chamber with a demonic statue inside, it has not been uncovered yet. And if it does exist, it most likely will not be denoted by a set of silver keys. While such keys are the symbol of a Pope, this use for them didn't come to pass until the late fifteenth century.

I hope this story has given you an enjoyable experience as we navigated the ancient (yet very recent) holiday of Halloween. For me, the joy of seeing my children light up when they don their favorite costumes and get far too much candy is priceless. This year my daughter was a character from the Netflix show *K-Pop Demon Hunters*, about which I know very little, though I can spot a tune from that movie a mile away now, and my son was a character from one of my very favorite movies – *The Sandlot.* Benny "The Jet" Rodriguez made an appearance in my neighborhood, complete with the pair of shoes that will make any kid the fastest in town, the P.F. Flyers.

If Halloween can bring magic into your world the same as it does for me, then I consider that worth celebrating indeed. Thank you for joining me on this journey. May your Halloween's always be spooky and filled with joy.

Andrew Clawson

February 2026

Excerpt from Saint Nicholas's Gold

You can get your copy of SAINT NICHOLAS'S GOLD on Amazon.

London

Twenty-five pieces of notebook paper for twenty-five thousand pounds.

Harry looked inside the hardcase folder at brittle pages, each encased in protective plastic. Scratchy handwriting ran along one edge of the front sheet. Notes, sketches and a few ink splatters. If he didn't know better Harry might think this was useless. Lucky for him he did know better. These pieces of scrap paper were worth more than a diamond mine.

"Congratulations, sir."

A bookseller who right now fancied himself the luckiest man in London shook Harry's hand one final time. "An excellent piece for your collection. Truly one of a kind."

That's what someone said after getting ten times their asking price for anything. The guy didn't know Harry would have paid ten times more. "Thanks." Harry tucked the folder under his arm and turned for the door. "Appreciate you opening the store late for me."

The bookstore's glass front door *dinged* as Harry pushed through it and stepped out onto Cecil Street. Bookshops lined the narrow alley on either side. Cecil Court was the premier shopping destination for bibliophiles in all of London. And, for tonight only, the best place for a relic hunter to find a treasure map. Perhaps.

He'd know soon enough. Harry turned his jacket collar up against the cold and headed into the middle of the alley. Streetlights turned the falling snow into a thin curtain on either side, the soft glow of closed shops throwing pockets of amber light onto the pavement while the wooden signs hanging above every door like tavern signs of old held onto the dusting of snow that landed atop them, some swaying in a gentle breeze, their gilt letters dulled at night. If it weren't for the cars parked on a cross-street ahead he could have been in this alley a hundred years ago, out to get the newest Sherlock Holmes story, released that week.

His footsteps echoed off the shop windows. No Conan Doyle for Harry tonight. His gut told him this wasn't a wild goose chase or a waste of time. The first draft under his arm – a first draft of a poem, of all things – was far more than a children's story. If his research was correct, these sheets of paper, the first attempt at what may be the most well-known story in America, were far more. They weren't a collection of rhyming lines and homely drawings. They were a treasure map, hidden in plain sight, a map no one knew existed. No one except Harry. And he knew how to read it.

A black taxi rolled past as he turned out of Cecil Court onto Charing Cross Road and walked into a wall of sound. The never-ending city soundtrack turned on with one step outside the narrow alley. Harry let out a breath. *That's more like it.* To a Brooklyn kid, it sounded like home. Which is where he was headed now. Sure, he'd paid twenty grand more than expected for this poem, thanks to whoever had been in the bidding war with him, but that guy lost and Harry won. Maybe Harry would find that guy after unraveling the truth behind this document and give it to him for free. If his suspicions proved true and luck was on his side, Harry would be able to afford it a million times over.

"Mr. Fox?"

The voice sounded from behind him. London accent, polite. Harry looked back and responded without thinking. "Yes?"

A fist slammed into Harry's nose. The blow spun his world and sent Harry down to one knee as the package tucked under his arm was ripped loose. One hand steadied him as Harry shook his head, fighting blurred vision and a supernova of hot pain to get a look at who had clocked him. A man, slender, with blonde hair long enough to be pulled back off his face. A *fast* man now running at full tilt away from Harry with the stolen pages under his arm. Harry pushed himself up. *Not so fast, pal.*

Pedestrians dotted the sidewalk as Harry raced around them and beneath bare tree limbs in pursuit of his quarry. How had the man known where to find Harry? What could he possibly want with the pages? Less important, who was he? These questions burst into his head as Harry skidded on a slick patch of sidewalk, bounced off a rubbish bin, and righted the ship. The speedy thief leaned into the turn as the road curved, a theater marquee and advertisements for a play flashing past as Harry hit the gas. A stoplight ahead turned green and the white police van with reflective yellow paint on the sides glowed as it motored away.

The thief turned left down a side street taking them into Covent Garden, past a towering statue and bustling pub, no one on the street giving much of a look at the two men locked in a breakneck race to parts unknown. A side street heading in the direction of the Thames was next, two pairs of footsteps echoing off the buildings to either side as Harry gained ground on the man. A man who knew what Harry had purchased, who had a reason to steal it, and who Harry should have seen coming. How dumb could he be? The bidding war. One other party had driven up the price of this poem tenfold at the very time Harry needed it. Only one reason made sense for such odd timing. The man knew its secret. He knew what it might contain. And he wanted it at any price.

Get the pages back now. Deal with the rest later. The alley ended ahead, the thief beating Harry out of it by mere steps before exploding through a tiny plaza packed with bicycles and a pair of buskers playing guitar. A four-lane road waited ahead. The speedy crook skidded into traffic and smacked into the side of an iconic double-decker bus letting someone off at the stop. He spun and took off down a walkway in the street's center, cars hiding him from view as they passed on either side. Harry waited for a gap in traffic before sliding through two oncoming vehicles to the sound of horns blaring and drivers cursing before he picked up the chase some twenty feet back of his quarry.

The Savoy Hotel flew by on his right, lights glittering and exotic cars idling outside the famous entrance. One of those sports cars, a garish canary yellow, pulled out in front of the thief as the Italian motor roared for freedom. Tires chirped, the thief jumped, and as the driver watched, the thief slid across the hood of his hideous vehicle and hit the ground on the other side without stopping. The man behind the wheel had his head turned to follow the crazed pedestrian as Harry went full tilt directly at the sports car, planting one hand on the roof and vaulting himself up and over to the far side. The roof barely reached above his waist. No problem clearing it. The width, however, was a problem.

The car never ended. He nearly made it to the far side when his feet hit the roof to upend Harry as he flew, flipping him up so he crash-landed on the far side. A string of profanity in a language he didn't understand burst from the car as he found his feet and took off. The thief was getting away.

They turned right at a major intersection and hurtled toward the Waterloo Bridge. Harry's lungs burned, his legs shouting for a break. This guy was some kind of marathon runner, gaining ground as the bridge onramp sloped upward slightly to make Harry's ragged breaths come even faster. A scooter zipped past, one of those small delivery ones, and Harry thought about stealing it from the driver before it zipped ahead.

The thief didn't think about stealing it. He did. The helmeted driver slowed to veer around the second crazy man running up a bridge. The thief pulled his stolen package back and whacked the driver alongside his helmet to send him flying off the motorbike. Noodles exploded over the road, the bike tipped over, and before Harry could gain any ground the thief had the bike upright and was motoring ahead to freedom. Harry slowed. *He's gone.*

A rumbling noise crept up from behind. The sort of noise you didn't ignore. Harry turned to find a double-decker bus barreling up the bridge in a bus-only lane. A lane with plenty of open space ahead, unlike the other lanes of traffic. Inspiration struck.

The bus came on him quickly. Harry put on a burst of speed as it passed, veering closer to the monstrous vehicle until the heat from its engine warmed his skin and the exhaust fumes burned his nose. A tiny bumper no wider than his foot protruded from the rear of the bus as it passed, inches from his swinging arm, slits in the metal engine cover shimmering as heat came out of them. This was going to hurt.

He grabbed the slits and jumped, pulling himself onto the narrow bumper as the rear of the bus went by, his fingers burning on the heated metal and a red taillight jamming into his face. His other hand slapped the red painted exterior. He scooted over until he could stand with one foot on the number tag and the other beside it, letting go of the searing metal to grab onto another taillight protruding from the rear. He latched onto the hard plastic and pulled himself against the bus.

A female passenger stared back at him from the rear window. She blinked and frowned. Harry grinned. The woman lifted a hand and waved.

The bus hit a bump. Harry went up with the bus, coming back down with a bang that nearly sent him to the pavement. He righted the ship and peered around the edge of the bus. Traffic to that side moved more slowly than in this lane. A motorbike ahead came closer as he watched. The helmetless driver did not turn around, strands of his blonde hair now flying wildly as he drove. Harry crouched. The burning metal on his hand would be nothing compared to hitting pavement at speed.

The bus slowed. So did the other lane of traffic. Brakes squealed, the bus came level with the bike, and Harry jumped.

Wind whistled as he soared above a metal traffic post that could split his head open, the pavement markings a blur and the lights of the towering London Eye spinning on the far bank as the helmetless thief stared ahead, never turning until Harry twisted his shoulder and smashed into the man, knocking him off the bike as Harry's world shuddered and his brain rattled in his head until nothing but chaos and fear remained.

The ground hit him like an uppercut. Harry landed atop the thief, who cushioned his fall but also acted like a springboard and bounced Harry up, twisting around so a second punch to the back knocked the wind from his chest as he crashed to the pavement again, bounced off a metal barrier and landed face-down in a pile of debris better left alone.

Shuddering concrete told him traffic approached. Stones bit into his palm as Harry pushed himself up with one hand, shook his head to clear the worst of it, then got to one knee. He looked ahead. The hardcase folder lay in front of him.

The pain vanished as he grabbed the folder and stood. He had it. Time to go. A car horn blared and he turned to find a black taxi racing toward him. Harry looked down. He was standing in middle of a lane of traffic. The barrier beside him had a metal railing across the top, so he put a hand on it and crouched, leaping up to vault over.

The thief crashed into Harry as he jumped. The folder went flying as the thief drove Harry into a sidewalk on the far side. A jogger leap over the two men and kept going as though nothing was amiss. The bridges outside wall kept them both from flying into the Thames, Harry ending up on the bottom of the pile with the thief on top. Not for long. Harry spun like the Tasmanian Devil from Looney Tunes and twisted free, hopping to his feet with his fists clenched in front of his face. The thief popped up with a grace Harry didn't like. The man didn't raise his fists. Instead, he smiled. Then he *laughed.*

"Almost, Mr. Fox." The English accent came through loud and clear.

Harry's answer was a left jab. The thief twisted to let Harry's fist slide past, one knuckle brushing the dapper mustache on the thief's upper lip. Too bad that left was a feint. The right cross caught him flush on the cheek and knocked him against the bridge wall. Harry turned to run, bending down to scoop up the folder as he did. He got hold of it, stood and went for the crashed moped that was now snarling traffic.

The thief kicked Harry's leg. It caught on his calf, sending Harry stumbling ahead. He never got his feet right before the thief crashed into him from behind. Their legs tangled, they lurched as one to the side, smacking into the barrier railing at full speed, a waist-high railing of metal pipe that hit the tornado of brawling humanity at just the wrong level. The two men tipped forward, Harry reaching for a railing he couldn't grab as their momentum threw him up and over the railing, the thief coming with him as their feet left the bridge and they tumbled over the side.

His stomach seized as Harry went weightless. He and the thief grabbed at each other out of sheer panic as they plummeted to the water below. How far down was it? He'd know soon enough.

Bang. A breath later Harry crash-landed. Not on water. On concrete. They'd plunged over the side and fallen directly onto a maintenance platform. No more than four feet wide, the metal floor had rails on one side that Harry smacked off when he landed and bounced. The thief clung to Harry until he shoved the villain aside, losing the folder as he did.

"Thank you." The thief had the folder. He got to his feet as Harry struggled up, nimble leapt down to landing below the platform, a landing the size of a pizza box, and disappeared into the bridge undercarriage. Harry's back shouted for a break as he forced himself up and gave chase. This guy was done for.

Traffic thundered overhead as the thief tiptoed long a structural service lip along a curving concrete lip which decorated the support pillar, grabbed a metal pipe with one hand and swung himself under the bridge and out of sight. Safety lights cast everything in a fearsome white. Icy wind coming off the Thames buffeted Harry as he followed the same path, the concrete vibrating with each step, forcing him to stop, chest pressed to the outside wall of the supporting archway as he scooted sideways until he ran out of service lip and jumped for the pipe. He caught it, dangled above nothing but air, then kicked himself forward and onto narrow strip of concrete spanning the underside of the bridge to connect two support arches.

The thief had vanished.

Harry's gut made him do it. He didn't think, didn't consider. He ducked.

The thief's fist flew above Harry's head, a blow thrown with such force that the villain stumbled forward, his knees crashing into Harry's back as he crouched down. Harry grinned. *Big mistake.* The thief's weight was over Harry when he wrapped an arm around the man's thighs, lifting him up at the same time he ripped the hardcase folder from the thief's grasp, holding it tight while he stood and hurled his adversary off the narrow concrete strip and into thin air. The man swiped for Harry's arm as he flew away. He missed.

Water flew in all directions when he splashed into the inky black River Thames. Harry leaned over, watching. A beat passed as the river moved on and the surface calmed. Movement from below disturbed the surface an instant before the man shot up, bobbing back down and using his arms to tread water. He whipped his head back to throw soaked hair out of his eyes and looked up.

Harry touched his forehead. The man laughed. Laughed so loudly it echoed off the underside of the bridge, the sound chasing Harry as he ran toward a maintenance ladder leading up to dry land. Harry shook his head. He couldn't help but admire the man. A thief, sure, and a man who knew a secret no one else should, but a man unlike any Harry had encountered. A proper villain.

As Harry climbed the steel ladder toward freedom, one question above all others stuck in his head. How did that guy know the secret about this poem? A secret, it now seemed, Harry needed to reveal without delay.

To continue the story, you can purchase a copy of SAINT NICHOLAS'S GOLD on Amazon.

***

GET YOUR COPY OF THE HARRY FOX STORY THE NAPOLEON CIPHER, AVAILABLE EXCLUSIVELY FOR MY VIP READER LIST

Sharing the writing journey with my readers is a special privilege. I love connecting with anyone who reads my stories, and one way I accomplish that is through my mailing list. I only send notices of new releases or the occasional special offer related to my novels.

If you sign up for my VIP reader mailing list, I'll send you a copy of The Napoleon Cipher, the Harry Fox adventure that's not sold in any store. You can get your copy of this exclusive novel by signing up at my website.

***

Did you enjoy this story? Let people know

Reviews are the most effective way to get my books noticed. I'm one guy, a small fish in a massive pond. Over time, I hope to change that, and I would love your help. The best thing you could do to help spread the word is leave a review on your platform of choice.

Honest reviews are like gold. If you've enjoyed this book I would be so grateful if you could take a few minutes leaving a review, short or long.

Thank you very much.

Also By

Also by Andrew Clawson

***

Harry Fox Origin Stories

The Midsummer Treasures

The All Hallows' Icon

Saint Nicholas's Gold

***

Harry Fox Adventures

The Arthurian Relic

The Emerald Tablet

The Celtic Quest

The Achilles Legend

The Pagan Hammer

The Pharaoh's Amulet

The Thracian Idol

The Antikythera Code

The Charlemagne Accord

The Centurion's Spear

***

The Parker Chase Series

A Patriot's Betrayal

The Crowns Vengeance

Dark Tides Rising

A Republic of Shadows

A Hollow Throne

A Tsar's Gold

***

The TURN Series

TURN: The Conflict Lands

TURN: A New Dawn

TURN: Endangered

About the author

Andrew Clawson is the author of multiple series, including the Parker Chase and TURN thrillers, as well as the Harry Fox adventures.

You can find him at his website, AndrewClawson.com, or you can connect with him on Instagram at andrew.clawson, on Twitter/X at @clawsonbooks, on Facebook at facebook.com/AndrewClawsonnovels and you can always send him an email at andrew@andrewclawson.com.

www.ingramcontent.com/pod-product-compliance
Lightning Source LLC
LaVergne TN
LVHW010703110826
845149LV00014B/3211
* 9 7 8 1 9 5 6 3 3 3 5 8 9 *